REVELATIONS

A TANNER NOVEL - BOOK 20

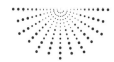

REMINGTON KANE

D1519479

Year Zero

INTRODUCTION

When an enemy delves into Tanner's past, they uncover long buried secrets that rock Tanner's world. The revelations usher in grief, as well as an unexpected joy.

THIS BOOK IS DEDICATED TO INNER CIRCLE MEMBER
MELODY WREST

PROLOGUE

STARK, TEXAS 1988

MARIAN PARKER MADE the turn off Main Street and headed up into the hills.

It was a blustery cold day and rain had begun falling in huge droplets. Marian didn't care. Inside, she felt as warm and radiant as a June day.

Her son, Cody, was in school, and Marian had left her three-year-old twin daughters with her best friend. The best friend was an older woman named Emily Sounder. At twenty-nine, Marian was a generation younger than Emily, but Marian had experienced the sort of childhood that made one grow up fast.

Despite their surface similarities and circumstances, Marian found she had little in common with women her own age.

Marian Parker understood the fragility of life and knew of its ability to alter in an instant. She never spent time on such frivolities as soap operas or bingo games. She was the

1

type of mother who read to her children nightly, grew her own vegetables, and expressed her love for her children both in words and deeds. Marian encouraged them toward becoming exceptional people.

Although her son, Cody, was at an age where young boys spent more time with their fathers than their mothers, Marian found that Cody still gravitated toward her. They talked often while out riding around their ranch. Marian treasured each moment she spent with her son.

Cody was a serious boy for his age, possessed of a will of iron, along with a streak of independence and a strong sense of self. Perhaps it was just a mother's pride, but Marian believed Cody to be highly intelligent and an original thinker.

It was not solely the sort of intelligence that would have him leapfrogging levels in school, rather, it was an emotional intelligence that would serve him well in life.

The men in Marian's family had a reputation for being strong-willed, daring, brave beyond measure, and unfortunately, cruel and ruthless.

She prayed nightly for Cody to be spared the negative traits that seemed to plague the male members of her family. She believed with all her heart that Cody possessed a core of goodness that would counterbalance any genetic tendency toward barbarism. Marian had nurtured that core of decency with love.

The sky darkened as the clouds thickened. Marian had planned to drive straight home with the twins after reaching Emily's house. Looking up at the sky, she thought that maybe she would just wait out the storm with Emily.

Marian had hit it off with Emily right away. Emily's children were grown and had moved to large cities. Emily's husband, Todd Sounder, had passed away two years earlier at the age of fifty-three. He had been felled by heart disease, although he'd been a thin man who neither drank nor smoked.

When it was your time to go, it was your time to go.

Marian brushed thoughts of Todd Sounder's sad fate from her mind and broke into another smile.

The rain increased as the wind continued its blustering. Marian was glad that she had only a few more miles until she reached Emily's house.

Her good mood seemed destined not to last. A huge pickup truck came up behind her fast, far too fast given the road conditions. Her smile faded as she gripped the steering wheel tight. The pickup truck was practically riding her bumper. Although daytime, it had grown dark, and the truck's lights were threatening to blind her.

Marian didn't dare pull over to the shoulder to let the truck pass. Given the amount of rain on the ground, she feared getting her tires stuck in mud. On the other side of the road was a wooden guardrail that bordered a sloping hill. The hill ended at a stream. Due to the rain, the stream would be flowing at a quick pace.

Marian white-knuckled her steering wheel while increasing her speed. She was hoping to build a gap between herself and the vehicle behind her. It didn't work. The pickup truck matched her increased speed and stayed on her bumper.

Marian beeped her horn to gain the driver's attention, then she made a waving gesture with her hand, telling the other driver to go around her. She was ignored. Marian began to suspect that the driver was staying close to her intentionally, and perhaps for no good purpose.

Just as that thought formed in her mind, the pickup truck swerved into the other lane and began passing her. When it was even with her vehicle, it matched her speed and stayed there. Marian tried to get a look at the driver, but the rain was coming down in a violent torrent that streaked her windows and tested her wiper blades. All she could tell was that her tormentor was male and had long hair.

Marian slowed, and the other vehicle slowed, she sped up again, and the truck fell back until she could see it in her rearview mirror. Along with that good fortune, came a lessening in the intensity of the rain.

A sigh of relief left Marian, until she realized she was traveling too fast and approaching a curve. Marian entered the curve while trying her best to slow down without losing traction and spinning out. As she made it around the curve she saw a sight that made her scream.

A large truck was headed for her. A truck going the wrong way on a one-way road while hogging the center line.

As alarming as that was, the expression on the truck driver's face was even more shocking. The man was grinning down at her, and he was someone Marian knew, someone from her past.

Marian swerved one way, then the other, but there was just not enough room to get by the truck.

~

HOURS LATER, Marian's husband, Frank Parker, gazed downward and watched with teary eyes as a rescue crew pried open his wife's mangled car, which had settled at the edge of the stream.

Frank had been told that Marian had burned to death inside the vehicle due to an electrical fire that had broken out in the car's interior.

The damn rain had failed to quench the blaze, because despite being cracked, Marian's windshield hadn't shattered to allow rain inside.

In the days ahead, Frank Parker would gain solace from

learning that his wife had died on impact from devastating head trauma, and that she never suffered the hell the blaze must have been.

A young widower, Frank would go on to live on the family ranch with his father, his two young twin daughters, and his son, a boy named Cody Parker.

The truth about Marian's "accident" wouldn't come to light for many years.

DIGGING INTO THE PAST

DANBURY, CONNECTICUT, 2017

ROBERT MARTINEZ SETTLED into his leather recliner and stared across at the middle-aged couple who were seated on his sofa. They were Mr. and Mrs. Barlow. At least, those were the names they were currently using. Martinez wondered what they hoped to gain by speaking to him.

He had agreed to the meeting after a former colleague at Hexalcorp assured him he would not be violating his parole by talking to them. He was also being paid for the interview. That had tipped the scales toward his agreeing to do it.

Neither Mr. Barlow, Michael, nor Mrs. Barlow, Kate, had ever been arrested for a crime. Martinez doubted that meant they had never been involved in criminal activities, only that they had never been caught by the authorities while doing so.

The same could not be said for Robert Martinez, who was known to have consorted with the late drug cartel leader Alonso Alvarado. The fact that Martinez had done so while working for Hexalcorp had been swept under the rug, along with Hexalcorp's other dark deeds.

The corporation was never investigated, thanks to large political contributions made to the right people. All blame for any misdeeds were placed squarely on Martinez's shoulders.

Because of the influence of his brother-in-law, Conrad Burke, Martinez had served only a year in a country club prison before being released to a decade of serving parole and having to check in once a month.

Overall, Martinez considered himself lucky. He had come very close to being killed in Mexico, and he had his holier-than-thou, billionaire brother-in-law to thank for his survival.

Michael Barlow was as average looking a man as Martinez had ever seen. The man stood about five-foot-ten and weighed somewhere around a hundred and seventy pounds.

Although handsome, the dark-haired man was not memorably so, while his brown eyes looked out at you from a clean-shaven face.

Kate Barlow matched her husband well, but they looked nothing alike. Kate had brown hair, gray eyes, and although she was lovely, she wasn't the sort of woman who would stay on your mind after only one meeting.

Michael was dressed in slacks with a sports jacket. Kate wore a dress with a hemline that was just above her knees. Their clothes spoke of a middle-class life style, of a home in the suburbs, and 2.3 children.

Martinez wondered if their appearance went a long way toward explaining their ability to fly under the law's radar.

Michael Barlow smiled at Martinez.

"Are you ready to begin the interview?"

"Sure."

"Good. Tell us everything you know about an assassin named Tanner."

Martinez's face grew pale.

"This is about Tanner?"

"Yes, we have a client who wants to know as much about the man as he can. It's our understanding that you researched Tanner extensively for Alonso Alvarado and have knowledge that we can use."

Martinez looked confused.

"I thought you worked for Hexalcorp? They have all my reports from that time period."

Kate Barlow shook her head.

"When your involvement with the Alvarado cartel came to light, Hexalcorp purged its files of anything having to do with the incident. Also, we don't work for Hexalcorp."

"If you don't work for Hexalcorp, then why was this meeting set up by a Hexalcorp employee?"

"That was a one-time thing," Michael Barlow said. "The black ops section of Hexalcorp is no more. It has become its own entity after forming an alliance with former members of a criminal organization called The Conglomerate."

"Tanner was involved in the destruction of The Conglomerate. He killed Frank Richards."

Michael Barlow nodded.

"We're aware of that. It seems Tanner's activities were in large part responsible for the formation of the current organization we're now working for as private contractors. If Tanner hadn't taken down The Conglomerate's leadership, Hexalcorp's black ops division would have had a much more difficult time morphing into its current form."

"What's the name of this organization?"

"They call themselves Ordnance Inc.," Kate Barlow said. "They hire out to whomever will pay as long as there is no conflict of interests between clients. Right now, they have a client who wants to know all there is to know about the assassin named Tanner. They contracted with us to gain that information. It's why we're here to see you, Mr. Martinez."

Martinez stood and walked over to the wet bar in the corner of his living room.

"Would either of you like a drink?"

The couple declined Martinez's offer. Martinez returned to his recliner with a whisky on the rocks. He hadn't really wanted the drink. He had wanted time to think. His ruminations had led him to the conclusion that he had information that was valuable and of greater worth than the pittance he had earlier agreed to accept.

After taking a sip of his drink, Martinez smiled at his guests.

"I know a lot about Tanner, including his real name. If you want me to talk I'll need more money."

Kate Barlow rose from her seat, walked over to Martinez's chair, then leaned over to stare into his eyes.

"My husband and I are carrots."

"What?"

"We're carrots. We come to see you, act polite, mind our manners, and when we leave you'll still be healthy and your home will be intact. There are other people that Ordnance Inc. might send to see you. Those people will be sticks. The sticks will hurt you in ways you've never imagined, then they'll burn your home to the ground for the hell of it. In either case, Mr. Martinez, you will reveal what you know about Tanner."

Martinez looked into Kate Barlow's gray eyes, before glancing over at her husband and meeting Michael Barlow's penetrating gaze. He was more certain than ever that the couple's outward appearance was a façade they put on for the world.

While they might not be violent, Michael and Kate

Barlow were ruthless professionals. They would brook no nonsense from him.

Martinez downed his drink as Kate resettled herself beside her husband. He then stood, poured himself a double whisky neat, and sat back in his recliner.

"I'll tell you everything I know about Tanner."

Kate Barlow smiled.

"How nice."

⁓

"WHAT DO you mean he's dead?" Michael Barlow asked.

Martinez held up a hand.

"Believed to have died, along with his whole family. It was Alonso Alvarado who murdered them."

"So, this boy, Cody Parker, he survived and grew up to become the assassin Tanner. Then, as Tanner, he went after Alvarado for killing his family?"

"Yes."

"How sure are you that any of the family is dead?"

Martinez shrugged.

"Alvarado told me that his men fired thousands of rounds into the Parker home, then firebombed it."

"Yes," Kate Barlow said. "But if the boy survived, perhaps his family did as well. If so, they could have gone into hiding under new identities."

"I guess anything is possible, but I doubt that's what happened," Martinez said. "Cody Parker survived his wounds, yes, but he was also spared the firebomb. Alvarado left him for dead outside the house."

Michael Barlow stood and paced for a few moments behind the sofa he had been sitting on. When he stopped walking, he leaned his elbows on the back of the sofa and spoke to Martinez.

"What about the mother, Cody's birth mother? What do you know about her?"

"Very little. Her name was Mary… Marilyn, something like that. She died in a car accident when Tanner was a boy."

"That's all you know about her? What about her maiden name?"

"Her maiden name was Gant. I only remember that because her father was that cult leader William Gant."

"I don't know that name," Michael said.

"I have a vague memory of hearing about William Gant," Kate said. "I may be wrong, but I think the serial killer Jeffrey Mitchell was his grandson."

Michael Barlow laughed.

"A cult leader and a serial killer. This Tanner has some genes in him. No wonder he's an assassin."

"What about Tanner's personal life?" Kate asked. "We understand that he's involved with an ex-FBI agent, but there must be someone in his past."

"Tanner killed Alvarado with the help of a woman named Alexa Lucia. One of Alvarado's investigators uncovered the fact that Tanner once went by another name, Xavier Zane. He was in his late-teens when he had that name and already working as an assassin. Under that identity, he was involved with a young woman, but we never learned her name or her fate."

"Was there any evidence that Tanner had ever married or had any children?" Michael Barlow asked.

"No, if he had a wife or a child Alvarado would have used them against him. However, Tanner and a woman named Laurel Ivy were lovers once. This occurred while the woman was married. Ivy is a medical doctor who had her license suspended because of a cocaine addiction. I also came across a rumor that Tanner sacrificed himself to save Laurel Ivy, but I never heard any details involving that. I do know Laurel Ivy is now married to the mobster Joe Pullo. Pullo and Tanner are also friends."

Kate smiled.

"This woman, Laurel, she may know something that could help us. Perhaps Tanner opened up to her in a way that he wouldn't do with anyone else."

Martinez snapped his fingers.

"I just remembered something about Tanner's mother."

"What is it?" Michael said.

"Tanner's father, Frank Parker. After he fired a ranch hand for being drunk, the man tried to make trouble for him with the law. The ranch hand claimed that Parker and his wife had faked her death to get insurance money. The man swore he had seen Marian, that's it, that was her name, Marian. Anyway, the ranch hand swore that he had seen Marian Parker a year or so after the accident."

"Was there an investigation?" Kate asked.

"Not really. It turned out that Marian Parker hadn't been insured. So, there was nothing for Parker to gain by faking his wife's death."

"What was the ranch hand's name?"

Martinez shrugged again.

"My memory isn't that good, but maybe you'll be able to find something in the public record. Although, I doubt it went as far as a formal investigation."

They spoke for another few minutes, but it became obvious that Martinez had told them all he knew about Tanner. The information was valuable and gave Michael and Kate Barlow a place to start.

~

THE COUPLE LEFT Martinez and returned to their car. Kate

climbed behind the wheel. She was an excellent driver and her husband avoided driving whenever he could.

"What's our next move?" Kate asked her husband as she drove away from Martinez's home.

"Laurel Pullo."

"Really? Do you think it's worth the risk of having a man like Joe Pullo gunning for us?"

"We won't go after his wife, but we need to figure out if she knows something about Tanner's family. After all, it's what we're being paid to do."

"It's beginning to look like the man has no family, at least, no close blood relations."

"Maybe, but we have to know for certain, and that story about his mother being alive intrigued me."

"Then we head to New York City?"

"Yes," Michael said.

Kate drove along West Street and headed for the entrance ramp to I-84.

2

MORE DIGGING

THE FOLLOWING EVENING, TANNER RODE THE PRIVATE elevator at Johnny R's strip club and stepped off to enter the reception area outside Joe Pullo's office.

He was met there by one of Joe's men, Big Ralphie, who sent Tanner a wave before pushing a button on the receptionist's desk.

Laurel Pullo came out of the office and greeted Tanner with a kiss on the cheek. She was wearing her blonde hair shorter during her pregnancy, since it made it easier to care for. Tanner pointed at her stomach and smiled.

"You've grown since I last saw you."

"And I'll grow some more. That's what pregnant ladies do."

Laurel peeked around Tanner.

"No Sara?"

"She stayed home."

"Good."

"She said you'd feel that way."

"I don't hate her, Tanner. I just don't think she's right for you."

"Most people think I'm wrong for her."

"I'm not most people."

"You can say that again," said Joe Pullo. Pullo swung the office door wide open and bid Tanner to join him. "Stop dogging Sara, Laurel, and let the man enter."

"I wasn't putting Sara down. I was just offering my opinion."

Pullo kissed his wife.

"I'll be home soon. I just have a little business to discuss with Tanner."

"All right, but I may go to bed early. Our flight leaves at ten a.m."

"It's scheduled for ten, but it leaves when we say so. It's a private jet," Joe said.

"I still like to be on time, and I can't wait to get there."

"Where are you two going?"

Laurel beamed with excitement as Pullo released a sigh.

"We're going to see Merle and Earl in Arkansas," Laurel said.

"Ah," Tanner said.

"Should I tell them you said hi?"

"No."

Laurel slapped Tanner on the arm.

"My brothers like you. They're scared of you, but they like you."

Laurel left with Big Ralphie at her side, while Tanner and Joe moved to the bar in the office to make drinks. They sipped on their whisky as they stood before a glass wall that looked down on the club. It was a busy night. Three girls danced on three different stages. Every table was full and the bar was deep with customers.

"You have work for me?" Tanner asked.

"No, but I wanted to let you know what's going on with Moss Murphy."

"More trouble?"

"No trouble, and that is the trouble. Moss Murphy isn't the type to let things go."

"Maybe not, but he has to be licking his wounds. I also promised to kill him if he didn't back off."

"Yeah, there is that."

"What about his son, Liam Murphy?"

"Moss must have shipped him off somewhere. No one has seen the kid in weeks. The only good thing to come out of that mess was Finn Kelly."

"He's working out?"

"Tanner, the man is worth his weight in gold. If I had more guys like him and Bosco I could run things with my eyes closed."

"How's Sammy doing?"

"He's more like his old self. He'll never be the happy-go-lucky kid he was, but he smiles once in a while."

Tanner nodded knowingly.

"What's the girl's name?"

Joe laughed.

"Yeah, there's a girl. Her name is Julie. She helps Laurel out at the clinic."

Down on the main floor, at center stage, was a brunette with the body of a goddess. Tanner pointed at her.

"Is she new?"

"Yeah, her name is Joy."

"I bet she brings them in here."

"Oh yeah. Should I introduce you?"

"Sweets like that are a no-no on my diet."

"You really are with Sara, aren't you? You know, I never thought you'd stay with one woman."

"I've done it before. It's just never worked out."

"And this time?"

"So far, so good."

Joe smiled.

"Me too."

~

LATER, as Tanner was leaving the club, the dancer he'd been watching walked up to him as he stepped off the rear doors of the elevator. Joy was standing in the corridor leading to the strippers' changing room. She was wearing a sheer red dressing gown that did little to hide her body.

"You're Tanner?"

"Yeah."

"Hi. I hear you're friends with the boss."

"That's right."

Joy looked him over, smiled, then leaned into Tanner and placed her arms around his neck.

"You want to be my friend too? I get off at midnight."

"You're very friendly, but I'll have to pass."

Joy narrowed her eyes.

"You're married?"

"No, but there's someone at home."

"I can keep a secret."

"I'll still have to pass, but I'm sure I'll dream of you tonight."

Joy laughed as she eased her arms from around Tanner's neck.

"Sweet dreams."

Tanner watched Joy until she disappeared behind the dressing room door. He took out his phone to call Sara.

"I don't have to work after all. Why don't we catch a movie somewhere?" After a pause to listen, Tanner smiled into the phone. "Yeah, I'll pick you up in ten minutes."

He left the club and headed for his car, with Joy all but forgotten.

∼

JOY PEEKED her head out of the dressing room a minute after Tanner left. When she saw that there was no one around, she headed for the metal door that led to the private rear parking lot.

Joy had discarded the dressing gown and was wearing an overcoat over her nakedness. Her face was still caked in the heavy makeup she wore for the stage.

After a short wait, a luxury car appeared outside the gate and parked across the street. Joy rushed to the gate and keyed in the code so she could leave the parking lot. Afterward, she crossed the street and went to the passenger side of the car.

∼

MICHAEL BARLOW LOWERED his window and smiled at Joy. Seated in the driver's seat, Kate Barlow wore a frown.

"We got your text," Michael told Joy. "I assume Tanner was unable to resist your obvious charms?"

"It was a no-go on the sex, but I still got his DNA."

Joy handed Michael a clear plastic envelope with a strand of hair inside it. She had plucked the loose hair off Tanner's shoulder.

Seated beside Michael, Kate made a face as she sighed.

"I suppose a hair is acceptable, but bodily fluids would have been better."

Joy looked worried.

"I still get paid, right?"

"Of course," Michael said, while passing Joy an envelope. "If you overhear anything around the club let us know."

Joy smiled at him, then she leaned over more, letting her coat gap open to grant Michael a view of her breasts.

"I hope I have a reason to call you," Joy said.

Michael watched Joy until she reentered the club. When he turned to look back at his wife, he found her scowling at him.

"What?"

Kate placed the car in gear.

"Put your eyes back in their sockets."

Michael laughed as he took out his phone. When he checked, he saw that he had a text message.

"Ah, I just received word from that researcher we hired. There was an allegation made against Tanner's father, Frank Parker, but as Martinez said, it went nowhere. The man who alleged Marian Parker was still alive is named Ronald Gowdy. His current address is in a suburb near Dallas."

"Do you think it's worth talking to the man?"

"I do, if only to dot every I and cross every T. I also have a feeling that there's something to the story."

Kate smiled.

"Oh, if we could deliver the whereabouts of Tanner's mother to the client we'd likely get a bonus."

"Yeah, if it's a close blood relative he wants, it doesn't get better than that."

"Still, you know he'll only use the woman as a way to torment Tanner."

"I assume that, but that shouldn't concern us. We were hired to do a job and we'll do it. End of story."

"I hope so. We're messing around with some dangerous people here."

"You mean Tanner?"

"Yes, and Joe Pullo too."

"We have nothing to fear from them. Besides, once we verify the existence of Tanner's close blood relative, we're out. What happens after that doesn't concern us."

"I still say we use extra caution on this one, and we'll need to change our identities again afterwards."

"What? But I like being Michael Barlow. I've been Michael Barlow for four years."

"No, we need to be careful. We'll get new names, then lay low for a while. You know, I've always wanted to see Brazil."

"Me too, so all right. We'll take a break after this."

"Good. Now tell me, what's next on the agenda?"

"We have to make travel arrangements and send this hair sample off to the lab, but we're free until tomorrow night."

"Great, then tomorrow we'll go to the museum."

Michael groaned.

"Do we have to? Museums are boring."

"You promised, remember?"

"Okay, but I get to pick where we go for dinner."

"No hot dog stands."

"Hardly. I've made a reservation for Maglione's."

"That place where all the Broadway stars eat?"

"Exactly."

They were stopped at a light. Kate leaned over and kissed her husband.

"Reservations at Maglione's makes up for you ogling that hooker, Joy."

"She's an exotic dancer, not a hooker. Men pay to look at her, not to touch her."

"She sells her body. In my book, that makes her a hooker."

Michael rolled his eyes.

"Whatever you say, dear."

3

MORE DIGGING, LITERALLY

THE FOLLOWING EVENING, KATE BARLOW STARED INTO THE storefront of a travel agency.

Featured in the display window were scenes showing Rio De Janeiro. Kate was mesmerized by the white sand beaches and the bluer than blue water. Her husband, Michael, stood beside her, and reached over to take her hand.

"It does look beautiful there, and I have to say, I've grown bored with Hawaii."

Kate laughed.

"I never thought I'd hear you say that. You've loved Hawaii ever since our honeymoon."

"Hawaii was a dream that came true. It's time for new dreams, new places."

"New people? Like that stripper?"

Michael released Kate's hand, then turned to face her.

"Are you serious? All I did was look at her."

Kate leaned in, stretched her neck upward, and kissed him on the lips.

"Of course, I'm kidding. I just like hitting your buttons sometimes."

Michael pulled her closer.

"I'll hit all your buttons as soon as we get back to our—" He stopped talking as he watched two men cross the street and head toward them. The men were young, both taller than he was, and they were heavily muscled. "Trouble," Michael said to his wife.

One man had dirty blond hair, while his partner was black. The black man appeared to be in charge. He spoke to them in an easy conversational tone.

"We're going to rob you, but we're not going to hurt you unless you make us. Hand over your wallets and phones and we'll be on our way."

Michael looked them over, as he did so, the blond man moved aside his jacket to reveal the silver pistol he kept tucked in his waistband.

"Just don't hurt us," Michael said.

Kate removed a phone from her purse, as Michael took one from an inside pocket of his jacket. The black man reached out to take the phone from Michael as his partner grabbed at Kate's. The two young thieves cried out in pain as they fell atop the sidewalk.

The "phones" hadn't been phones at all, rather, they were cleverly disguised stun guns. The gadgets worked well, but didn't pack the punch of their more traditional units. The two men recovered within seconds, but by then, Michael and Kate had taken their weapons.

The blond man's gun turned out to be an old Bersa Thunder. The gun had a profile similar to a Walther PPK, but cost less. The black man had a Glock 19. Kate examined the weapon and saw that the Glock was well-maintained and fully loaded. After brushing a finger across the gun's extractor and finding it flush, she assumed there was also a round chambered.

The black man stood slowly, then helped his partner up.

They were still shaky from th[...]
dangerous nonetheless.

"I say we shoot them both in t[...]
wasn't serious, and had to keep hersel[...]
she saw the blond man's knees buckle a bi[...]

Michael looked thoughtful.

"I don't know. This neighborhood does[...]
traffic, but we still might be seen by someone, and[...]
an awful racket."

"You don't have to shoot us," the blond said. "We w[...]
gonna hurt you."

"Fair enough," Kate said. "Then give us your wallets an[...]
phones."

"What's that?" the black man asked.

"You heard her," Michael said. "Your wallets and your
phones, right now."

The black man laughed.

"Shit. I thought you were a couple of dumbass tourists,
but you two are something else." He handed over his phone,
then shrugged. "I never carry ID while I'm working."

The blond man had a wallet, along with an iPhone.
Michael noticed that the black man's phone was a
throwaway that he'd never miss, and which couldn't be
connected back to him. He offered the man some advice.

"You should lose your partner, and go after bigger game
too. You're past the mugger stage."

The black man smiled. He was younger than Michael had
first assumed, and likely not yet twenty. Although Michael
and Kate had the upper hand, the kid seemed calm.

The blond man was sweating and panting. He kept eyeing
the gun Michael had taken off him.

Michael stared at him.

"Why don't you run along, Blondie."

"I can go? Really?"

backward glance,
ate.

e gun he was
his phone." He

Trevor you

does a little
always looking for smart
cards right and you'll be making good

Kate gave Marcus back his phone. She then emptied his gun of ammo and handed it back to him.

"We're Kate and Michael. Trevor will know us."

Marcus laughed as he put away the phone and the gun.

"This might be my lucky night. Thanks, and will I see you two around if this Trevor guy takes me on?"

"You just might, Marcus," Michael said. He handed Marcus the wallet and phone he'd taken from his partner. The wallet only had twelve bucks in it.

"You two are all right," Marcus said. He sent the couple a smile, then walked off.

Kate leaned over and whispered to her husband.

"That was nice of you."

Michael shrugged.

"We got breaks when we were young and inexperienced. Why shouldn't he get the same?"

Kate laced her arm through her husband's and they walked around the corner, crossed the street, and went right at the next intersection.

A minute more and they were breaking into the townhouse owned by Joe Pullo.

~

STARK, Texas, Two Days Later, 2:17 a.m.

KATE PULLED on the scarf she wore around her neck to make it tighter, in an effort to ward off the chill of the night air.

Her husband stood beside her as they watched their assistants dig up the graves of the Parker family. Michael Barlow had insisted on being present while the work was going on.

They were on the Reyes' Horse Ranch, which was formally The Parker Ranch and the childhood home of Cody Parker, of Tanner.

The men desecrating the graves were members of Ordnance Inc. Their team consisted of a leader, code-named Alpha.

Alpha arrived with ten other men and one woman whose various code-names were as follows: Bravo, Charlie, Delta, Echo, Foxtrot, Golf, Hotel, India, Juliett, Kilo, and Lima.

The men all wore beards, some of which were phony. They normally dressed in suits with red ties and wore mirrored sunglasses, but tonight's attire was coveralls, work boots, and headlamps.

Alpha, their leader, supervised, while Juliett, the lone woman in the group, helped out where needed by handling tools and passing out bottles of water.

Alphas were always Alphas, however other team members names could and would change depending on when they were picked for an assignment.

The goal of this assignment was to get in and get out as

REMINGTON KANE

soon as possible after obtaining DNA from each of the seven corpses buried in the small family cemetery.

The graves were those of Frank Parker, his first wife Marian Parker, his second wife Claire Parker, and his four children, Cody, Jessica, Jill, and James. The bodies of Cody Parker and Marian Parker would be removed and taken to a private lab.

Kate maintained her composure during the extraction of material from the adult corpses, including the one purporting to be the body of sixteen-year-old Cody Parker. Then, the bodies of the young twin girls were violated, and Kate's mouth formed a grim line. When the baby's body was unearthed, Kate let out a whimper, but it was soft and heard only by her husband.

Michael Barlow took his wife's hand.

"It's almost over."

"When will we get the DNA results back?"

"Trevor says it's a priority and they've already begun work on the hair obtained from Tanner. Trevor should be able to give us the results very soon. If, as we suspect, Tanner is Cody Parker, and if, as we hope, one or more of these other bodies doesn't match genetically, then we'll know that Tanner has a blood relative out there somewhere."

"A blood relative we have to track down, which could take some time."

Michael smiled at his wife.

"That's why we're well paid for what we do."

"You're hoping that the body in Marian Parker's grave doesn't match the DNA of the others. So am I after talking to Ronald Gowdy."

~

MICHAEL AND KATE had spoken to Ronald Gowdy over

breakfast in an eatery in Dallas. The reformed alcoholic was one of the fittest looking sixty-somethings that Michael had ever seen.

Gowdy was positive that he had seen Marian Parker alive and well a year after she had been said to have died.

When asked why he was so positive that it was Marian Parker he had seen, Ronald Gowdy blushed a shade, then smiled.

"I had the hots for that woman. Most of us ranch hands did. And then there were those eyes of hers. Those eyes would be scary on a man, but with Marian... hmm, boy. I'll tell you, every time she looked my way my knees grew weak."

"What was it about her eyes?" Michael had asked.

"They were intense. When Marian looked at you, even a casual glance, it was like she was staring at you, into you. Believe me, having a woman that hot stare at you is a turn-on."

"Have you ever seen her again?" Kate asked.

"No, but I saw her that day. I swear it. That woman was still alive a year after they said she had died."

Michael and Kate thanked Gowdy and left him a way to leave a message in case he remembered anything else.

∾

"THAT OLD LADY certainly was no help," Kate said. She was referring to Emily Sounder. The Barlow's researcher discovered that Emily Sounder had been Marian Parker's best friend. After speaking with Ronald Gowdy, Michael and Kate went to talk to Emily.

The old woman still lived in Stark, Texas. They approached her under the guise of being writers who were looking into the history of Stark. When they learned about the massacre that had taken place at the Parker Ranch, they decided to do a little background research on the family. That led them to Emily.

Emily Sounder had been polite to the couple but only told them what they already knew. Marian Parker had died during a rainstorm after losing control of her vehicle. When she was asked about the allegation made by Ronald Gowdy, the disgruntled ranch hand fired by Frank Parker, Emily pleaded ignorance.

"I never knew such a statement had been made. If so, it was all a lie. Poor Marian is dead, long dead."

The couple thanked the old woman for her time and left her neat little house.

Hours later, they stood watching a crew from Ordnance Inc. desecrate graves.

The work took longer than expected, but was completed well before dawn. They left the graves exposed. It was more important to avoid a confrontation than it was to cover their tracks.

Kate drove them back to their hotel as her husband slept in the passenger seat.

She didn't like this assignment, but Ordnance Inc. paid well, was professionally run, and guaranteed their anonymity.

Once they could supply the client with the name and location of Tanner's blood relative, they would be done. They could take a long vacation in Rio and recharge their batteries.

And yet, Kate wondered if it would be that easy.

Kate had no doubt that their client wanted the name of Tanner's family member in order to use that person against the man, to use them either as bait or to possibly harm them in retribution.

Tanner's reputation made him out to be a ruthless and formidable man. If he came out on top, might he not look for any other parties that were involved, such as Kate and her husband?

The thought made Kate shiver more than the unearthing of the graves had.

They were committing atrocities against a man who would kill them without blinking an eye.

Kate reached over into the passenger seat and shook her husband, to rouse him from sleep.

Michael cleared his throat as he sat up and looked around. There was only darkness beyond the illumination of their car's headlights.

"What's up?" he asked

"I want you to get those new identities ready as soon as possible. We need to be able to disappear the second this job is done."

"You're worried about Tanner?"

"I'm worried about Tanner."

"I ordered the new ID's yesterday. Three sets of new ID's, complete with passports."

"Three sets?"

"Just in case. We'll use one set to get to Rio, then once there, we'll use another set. That should throw anyone looking for us off our trail. If it doesn't, we'll still have a set left to use."

Kate took her eyes from the road and studied her husband's face.

"Tanner worries you too, doesn't he?"

"Yes, but he won't spend his life tracking us down. If we make it difficult for him to find us, he'll accept that we escaped his reach. After all, we're not going after the man personally. We're just the hired help."

"And what about Pullo?"

"What about him? We searched his place and left everything as we found it."

"Except for that picture. Lauren Pullo had a picture of Cody Parker and his mother. What if she realizes it's missing?"

Michael shrugged.

"So what? Who would break in and take just that photo? She'll assume she misplaced it. It could be years before she misses it. Pullo will not be a problem."

"I guess you're right."

~

DAYS LATER, Michael's phone rang as Kate was at the door of their hotel room accepting their breakfast from room service.

The call was from the man heading the operation for Ordnance Inc., Trevor Healy. Healy had the results of the DNA tests.

Michael listen attentively to Trevor's news, then made a suggestion.

"We need to know more in order to track our subject. I suggest a Hammer Team be sent to interrogate the woman we spoke of in our last conversation."

Michael heard Trevor laugh at his suggestion. An Ordnance Inc. Hammer Team consisted of eight members, most of whom have been in combat. Every one of them was highly-trained, ruthless, and disciplined. The eight team members always included a woman in the mix, and they were always beautiful women.

The women were used as distractions, as lures, and as spies.

"I don't think a Hammer Team is necessary. After all, she's just one woman."

"I understand, Trevor, but our research has uncovered the fact that she's resourceful and capable of killing."

"Understood, but I think a three man team will work. I'll hire a group of locals and contact you when we have more info."

"Okay, we'll be standing by."

Michael ended the call and found Kate staring at him.

"What's happened?"

"The body that was in Cody Parker's grave is definitely not Cody Parker, and it's the wrong nationality. Furthermore, the body removed from Marian Parker's grave is not a match to the twin girls."

"So, you were right?"

Michael grinned.

"Tanner's mother, Marian Parker, she's alive."

4

A FELLOW TEXAN

THE FOLLOWING MORNING IN MANHATTAN, TANNER SPOTTED
Finn Kelly while running in Central Park along the Reservoir
Loop.

Tanner had just begun his run. It appeared Kelly was
doing the same. Tanner saw the man finish a series of
stretching movements, then take off running.

Finn Kelly ran his miles with the same intensity that
Tanner devoured his own. Tanner quickened his pace until
he drew even with Kelly and sprinted along beside him.

Finn Kelly greeted Tanner with a smile. The Irishman
wore black sweatpants along with a black sleeveless T-shirt.
Tanner was dressed similarly, although his T-shirt had
sleeves.

Kelly's arms were muscular and defined, but not large.
Although he was running at high speed, there but a
slight sheen of perspiration on Kelly's brow.

The two men ran together in silence, but as they
approached the point where Tanner had first spotted him,
Kelly asked Tanner a question. Although he was running fast,

and had been doing so for a while, Kelly's voice was normal and he showed no sign of being tired.

"You fancy another go-round?"

"Yeah," Tanner said. "And then I'll buy us breakfast."

"I'll take that deal."

The two men began their second lap around the six-mile track. They passed the slower runners with ease while eliciting astonished glances from many of them.

They came to a stop after well over an hour of running and stared at each other. Although they were both breathing hard, neither man was gulping in air or dripping sweat.

"I see you're in great shape, Tanner."

"No more than you are."

"It pays in our occupations. Sometimes you win by simply outlasting the other man, or men."

They left the park and walked two blocks to a deli.

Kelly's appetite surprised Tanner. The man devoured an omelet, two orders of toast, and a thick slab of ham, then followed it with a piece of apple pie.

Tanner enjoyed his own omelet, but passed on the ham and had an egg bagel instead of toast. As they ate, Kelly told Tanner that he liked working for Joe Pullo, and that he was surprised when the man gave him so much responsibility.

"I give you credit for that, Tanner. You took a chance and trusted me, so Pullo did the same."

"Joe says you're good at what you do, better than good, and that's rare."

They concentrated on their food, but spoke more over their second cups of coffee. Tanner was surprised to learn that Finn Kelly had started life in Texas.

"I thought you were born and bred in Ireland?"

"Bred there, yes, but I was born in a town named Bando, Texas."

Tanner sat up straighter. Bando was a neighboring town to the east of where he'd grown up in Stark, Texas.

"How old were you when you moved away?"

"Barely three, or so they tell me. My parents died in a train accident and my Aunt and Uncle came and took me back to Ireland. My mother was an American, my Father came from Dublin. I was told my mother had no relatives, but I've no idea if that was true. The woman was a bit of a mystery."

"What do you mean by that?"

"When I came back to this country I decided to see if I had any family here from my mother's side. When I looked into my mother's background I found almost nothing. My guess is that she was using a phony name. For what purpose, I don't know. Perhaps she was on the run from a violent husband when she met my father. I only have one picture of my parents. They're smiling like teenagers in the photo. I like to remember them that way."

Tanner reciprocated in the conversation and was surprised to find himself opening up to Kelly.

He liked the man. There was something about Kelly. He was no saint, nor was Tanner, but Tanner sensed an honorable streak in the Irishman. Although Finn Kelly might commit violent acts, he would never perform them out of viciousness or to get a sick thrill.

Violence would be work to Kelly, or done as a necessity, just as it was for Tanner.

"I grew up in Texas," Tanner said.

Kelly shook his head.

"You don't sound like it. Did you leave there when you were young?"

"I was sixteen. Since then I've traveled a lot."

Kelly spoke to Tanner in French.

"Yes, I speak French, and several other languages."

"That's good to know. I speak French, German, and a little Italian. If I ever need to say something to you in private, I'll say it in German."

Tanner laughed.

"Joe's right. You are good. You plan ahead even when there's no need."

Kelly stood and threw down money to cover the tip.

"Thanks for breakfast, Tanner. I'll see you around."

"Right," Tanner said. He watched Kelly hail a taxi, then paid the bill and left the restaurant.

After walking six blocks, Tanner checked his watch and saw that he was still early for his meeting. That was good.

He trusted the man he was meeting, at least to a degree, but it was just good sense to check your surroundings before arriving somewhere you were expected to be.

Once he was satisfied that no one was watching the café, Tanner entered and ordered a third cup of coffee. The man he was there to meet was named Duke. Duke was a supplier who sold unusual or illegal items.

To Tanner's surprise, Duke waved to him in greeting from a back room of the café. Tanner entered the small room cautiously, then saw the bank of cameras that displayed the café and the streets surrounding it.

"You have a connection to this place, Duke?"

"I bought it. I was tired of meeting clients in bars."

"I guess you spotted me coming."

"And we'll spot anyone else coming, like cops. If that happens, I know a hidden way out of here."

Tanner looked at the table that was in front of the bank of cameras. Duke had several items there, including a pair of eyeglasses with wide lenses.

Duke saw where Tanner was looking. He picked up the glasses, then pointed toward a small powder room.

"These work like a disguise. There's a mirror in that bathroom. Try on the glasses and tell me what you think."

"Eyeglasses? That's not much of a disguise."

Duke grinned.

"You'll see."

Tanner took the glasses from Duke. They seemed heavier than they looked. When he tried them on and gazed in the mirror, he was shocked by how different he appeared.

His intense eyes seemed tamer, while the shape of his face looked wider, and his brow lower. Tanner moved his head to the left, then the right, in profile, the effect was lessened, but still there.

"What are these?"

"Light-refracting lenses. There's a whole scientific explanation about why they work, but all I know is that they change your looks. They were designed to counteract facial recognition software, and they do, but only about ninety percent of the time."

Tanner asked how much they were and was surprised at the cost. After considering it for a moment, he decided the glasses were worth the money.

"Take ten-percent off that price and I'll buy two pair."

"I can do that, but I'll need time to come up with a second pair. My supplier is a former toymaker for the CIA. He's gone out on his own and has a lot of unusual goodies."

Tanner picked up a sound-suppressor. It was very thick, but short.

"That's a free sample," Duke said. "My guy says it's as quiet as a whisper, but it's only good for one use. If you like it, I'll get more."

Tanner pocketed the silencer, then pointed at a cell phone. "What's that do?"

"It works like a stun gun. There are cheap ones on the

market in the spy shops, but this one will put a guy's lights out for several minutes, not just stun him."

"I'll pass. If the spy shops are selling it, they'll soon be common knowledge and become useless." As he moved along the table, Tanner looked down at a silver case. "What's in there?"

"Tracking devices. They're tiny, but work up to a hundred miles."

"How do they attach?"

"In two ways, adhesive or magnetic."

"I'll take them," Tanner said, after hearing the price. He also bought miniature explosives, along with other exotic toys.

Duke looked pleased.

"I thought you'd like my new suppliers' stuff."

"If the silencer works like he says, I'll buy more. It's tough to find a good sound suppressor."

Tanner used his phone to send money to Duke's account, then left the café wearing the glasses. They didn't affect his vision and he wanted to get used to wearing them. They would come in handy in his false identity of Thomas Myers.

Tanner checked the time on his phone after hailing down a taxi. He had another meeting to attend, or rather, Thomas Myers had to sit through a meeting of the condo board at his new residence.

Several tenants had been miffed at Thomas Myers being approved for the penthouse apartment without being vetted by the condo board. There were also complaints about the noise that had gone on during a renovation while Tanner was away in Wyoming visiting Spenser.

The condo had been made more suitable for Tanner's needs. This included turning a room into a sound-proofed shooting range. The work had cost Tanner a small mint, but given that the apartment was payment for past work, he was well ahead.

Sara loved the apartment, so Tanner was willing to put up with the pomposity of his hoity-toity neighbors. Despite their complaints, the apartment was his.

As Thomas Myers, he would smile and seek to placate them. If anyone became too annoying, well, perhaps he'd find out just how silent his new silencer was.

Tanner arrived at his new home and headed for the shower. A note from Sara informed him that she would be back soon from her breakfast with her sister.

After showering, Tanner donned a conservative suit, along with his new glasses. It was time to play Thomas Myers.

5

A NEW ENEMY

MICHAEL AND KATE BARLOW SAT ON A PARK BENCH IN STARK, Texas. They watched as two large men walked toward them.

"They look exactly as I expected them to look," Kate said. Michael nodded in agreement.

Kate had been referring to Ernie and Rich Harvey.

The two brothers were the local tough guys in Stark. They made their living selling weed, and occasionally cocaine.

The Harvey brothers had an agreement with the police. Keep the hard drugs out of Stark and we'll leave you alone. It was a good arrangement.

Stark stayed the same small town it had always been and Ernie and Rich had fun breaking the bones of any would-be rival dealers.

It didn't hurt that they gave free weed to the cops, or that they had gone to school with most of them.

The Harvey brothers' names had come up after Ordnance Inc. sent out the word that they would pay for any info anyone in Texas had concerning Tanner.

Tanner had tangled with the Harvey brothers during his

last visit to Stark. Michael and Kate were excited by the fact that Tanner, who they now knew for certain was Cody Parker, had recently returned to Stark for a short time. Perhaps the man had been in the area visiting someone, such as his mother.

~

"YEAH, Tanner was here about two years ago. He was staying at the Reyes Ranch," Rich Harvey said.

Michael and Kate Barlow smiled at each other. It seemed that Cody Parker had returned home.

"This woman, Maria Reyes, what does she look like?" Michael asked.

"She's a good-looking woman for her age, you know the type?" Ernie said, while eyeing Kate.

"Is she white?" Kate asked.

"Nah, she's a Mex," Rich said.

"Have you ever seen an older white woman staying at the ranch?" Michael asked.

Both brothers sent him a shrug.

"It ain't like we hang around there," Rich said. "But Stark is a small town, I don't remember any strangers being here lately except for you two."

Michael and Kate asked a few more questions, but it was obvious that the Harvey brothers knew little, other than the fact that Tanner had once returned to Stark.

After paying the brothers for their time, the couple left the park and got back in their car.

"Where to next?" Kate asked.

"Head to Brownsville. We're meeting Trevor Healy there."

"Why Brownsville?"

"Trevor will be overseeing another operation from there."

Kate started the engine, but before she could place the car in gear, a ringing sound came from her purse.

"My phone is set to vibrate. That must be the phone we're using for contacts on this job."

Kate looked at the phone and smiled.

"It's Ronald Gowdy. Maybe he remembered something new."

"Or better yet, he spotted Marian Parker again," Michael said.

Kate answered and listened as Ronald Gowdy talked. She only spoke three times. Twice she asked a question, then ended by telling Gowdy he would receive more money and to call if he remembered anything else. After putting the phone away, Kate filled in her husband.

"Mr. Gowdy thinks Marian Parker may have been working as a nanny. He remembered that she was holding a baby when he saw her."

Michael made a clucking sound with his tongue.

"This gets weirder and weirder. Why would the woman fake her death to leave her husband and children, then turn around and get a job as a nanny?"

"There's no history of domestic abuse in the home. From everything we've gathered, Marian Parker had a good marriage and was a wonderful mother. Still, I have an idea about the nanny theory."

"Yes?" Michael said.

"What if the child was hers? If so, then Tanner might also have a sibling out there somewhere."

Michael laughed.

"Let's hope you're right. That will give the client two targets of opportunity."

Kate put the car in drive and headed toward Brownsville, Texas.

~

TANNER'S BUILDING kept a meeting room on the ground floor.

He entered it with Sara at his side and looked around. The small room was crowded, but not packed tight. Conversations lost volume or ceased at his appearance.

Tanner was wearing a blue suit along with the light-refracting glasses. Sara told him he looked like a bank executive. She was startled by the changes the glasses made to his face and agreed that the lenses soothed his fierce gaze.

A man rushed toward them from the front of the room. He was the condo president, Walter Jenson. Jenson had used his authority to get Tanner into the building. He was not aware of who Tanner was, but only that he was a friend of Joe Pullo's.

Jenson also looked like a banker. He had been one for over forty years before retiring. While at the bank, he had laundered millions for the Giacconi Family. In return, the late Sam Giacconi had rescued Walter Jenson from facing an embezzlement charge that would have seen him go to prison for many years.

Jenson was sixty-six, looked trim, and was tall. His hair was streaked with white, while his nose was red from drink. Jenson drank a lot, but rarely to the point of drunkenness. The vice was offset against Jenson's habit of playing tennis nearly every day.

Tanner shook Jenson's offered hand after the man mentioned how different he looked with glasses on. He then watched as the man's admiring eyes took in Sara.

Sara wore a simple green dress that displayed her shapely legs while maintaining her modesty. Her lustrous black hair was loose and it shined beneath the lights in the ceiling.

"Mr. Myers, Miss Blake, thank you for attending the meeting."

"Who is here that has a problem with me?" Tanner asked.

Jenson's gaze went to the front of the room where an Asian man in a three-piece suit was staring back at them.

"That's Eric Tang. He owns the Buy-Rite appliance stores. He's angry that he didn't get the penthouse. He really wanted the penthouse."

"How many condo members does he have on his side?"

"I'd say about eight of them. They hate the fact that the rules were written so that I could override the board. Nonetheless, that's the way things are, so they really have no way to redress what they perceive as an injustice."

"I get that," Tanner said, "and I'll handle it."

As they walked toward the front of the room, Sara whispered to Tanner.

"What do you plan to do?"

"Shoot them."

Sara laughed.

"That seems to be your usual plan, but you might want to try a different approach while you're pretending to be mild-mannered Tom Myers."

"I'll speak their language, which is money and self-concern."

As they approached him, Eric Tang stepped forward and blocked their path. He looked Tanner over from head to toe while scowling, but then he offered Sara a gracious smile.

"Mr. Myers, Miss Blake, my name is Eric Tang."

Neither Tanner or Tang offered their hands to each other, but Sara put hers out, and Tang took it.

"It is a pleasure to meet you, Miss Blake," Tang said, before sending Tanner a look that told him he was displeased by his very existence.

Tang was the same height as Tanner, but ten years older.

He had a military bearing about him that was accentuated by his close-cropped hair. He spoke with a slight British accent.

Tang's suit was well-tailored and revealed that Tang was in good shape. The dark eyes bore into Tanner's and a staring contest began. The animosity in Tang's gaze turned into curiosity. He had seldom met a man who could withstand his steely gaze.

Sara cleared her throat and Tang glanced at her.

"Are you married, Mr. Tang?"

"Yes, Miss Blake. However, my wife and children are visiting her parents in London."

"I would love to meet her someday."

"Perhaps that will happen," Tang said. There was a small knot of people gathered behind Tang. He gestured at them. "These tenants, along with myself, have concerns about your occupancy of the penthouse, Mr. Myers. We intend to voice our displeasure at the decision."

"I see," Tanner said.

Tang stepped aside and Tanner and Sara joined Walter Jenson at the front of the room.

Jenson stood before a podium, then raised his voice to gain everyone's attention and settle them down.

"Thank you all for coming. I'd like to introduce you to Mr. Thomas Myers and Miss Sara Blake. They're our newest neighbors."

There was a smattering of applause mixed with muttered grumbling. It died quickly when Tanner took Jenson's place at the podium and stared out at the crowd.

On the whole, the men were older than himself, although many of their wives seemed younger. One man was seated in a wheelchair beside a blonde no older than Sara, although the man had to be pushing eighty. For the blonde's sake, Tanner hoped the man was her grandfather.

Tanner smiled at the gathering. He was trained and

experienced in role camouflage. Being Thomas Myers was just one more role to play.

"It's good to meet you all. Sara and I hope to become friends with you and, in that spirit, we have a gift to offer you."

Tanner reached inside an inner pocket and brought out a check, which he handed to Walter Jenson. The condo board president's eyes grew wide as he read the notation written on the check.

"Ladies and gentlemen, Mr. Myers has just graciously donated the needed funds to complete the renovation of the building's pool."

Tanner had become aware that the board had been promising for over a year to repair and upgrade the building's community pool. They had only reached a fraction of the money they needed. The new tenant, Tom Myers, had just filled the gap.

Tanner leaned over and whispered to Jenson, whose smile widened.

"Mr. Myers will also fund a play zone for the children in the building."

Tang spoke up.

"A play zone? And just where will we find the square footage to place it?"

"I consulted an architect," Tanner said. "She assured me that a play zone could be constructed in the space above the swimming pool. Your children and the children of the other tenants will have a place to go on rainy days."

The crowd was quiet for a moment, but then the clapping began.

The blonde raised her hand as if she were still in high school. When Tanner pointed at her, she sent him a dazzling smile.

"I'm Sylvia, Mr. Myers, and this is my husband, Harvey

Anderson. On behalf of everyone I'd like to thank you for your generosity, but I do have a question."

"Yes?" Tanner said.

"When will the pool be ready for use? It's been ages since I've gotten wet."

Tanner stared at her while wondering if Sylvia's words had a double meaning. Sara certainly took it that way. Tanner saw that Sara was staring daggers at the shapely blonde.

"I'll leave the details up to the condo board," Tanner told Sylvia Anderson. He looked over at Eric Tang and saw that the man was already gazing his way.

The group that had been ready to support Tang were now talking excitedly among themselves about the pool Tanner was funding. Their grievance against Thomas Myers was forgotten. They would soon have a place in the building where they could spend time with their children and grandchildren. That made Tom Myers all right in their book.

Tang mouthed the words, "Well played."

Tanner sent him a slight nod of acknowledgement, but knew he had an enemy in the building.

That was fine. Unlike most of his enemies, Tang wouldn't send an army of thugs after him. At least, Tanner hoped not.

6

WHO ARE THEY?

LATER THAT NIGHT, TANNER WAS AT JOHNNY R'S, INSIDE JOE Pullo's office.

The two men were seated at the small wet bar Joe kept in the office. Joe was on Tanner's left, and had just informed Tanner that his brownstone had been broken into.

"Who would be stupid enough to rob you?" Tanner asked.

"This wasn't done by fools. They left almost no trace that they had been there. They bypassed the alarm system and even hacked into the security cameras' files."

"You say 'they.' It was more than one?"

"A man and a woman, judging by their silhouettes, but they were masked and wore gloves. I wouldn't know that much, but Finn Kelly retrieved their images from the cameras' backup files in the cloud storage."

"Where did they slip up?"

Pullo smiled.

"I'm old school, Tanner. Cameras and alarms are great, but I still leave a hair in the doorjamb when I go away. I noticed the hair was gone before I ever checked the cameras."

"Smart. But what did they take? They must have taken

something... or left something. I hope you checked for explosives?"

"Yeah, along with recording devices and toxic substances. The place is clean. They only took one item. It was a picture of you that Laurel had. The one that was taken when you were a kid."

Tanner stiffened atop his stool and turned his head to stare at Joe.

"So, you know?"

"Yeah, your real name is Cody Parker. After you went to Mexico and killed him, I figured out that sonofabitch Alonso Alvarado was the one who murdered your family."

"When did Laurel tell you she had the picture?"

"On our honeymoon. Laurel didn't want me to think she had any secrets where you're concerned."

"That makes sense," Tanner said, before downing the rest of his drink.

"Somebody is looking into your past, Tanner. What I can't figure is why, unless you have some family left somewhere."

"There's no one other than cousins I recently met. My immediate family all died years ago. If someone was looking to hurt me that way they're out of luck."

"Any idea who might be behind the break-in? Chances are good that the thieves were hired help."

Tanner looked down at the carpet as he thought things over. When he lifted his gaze, he stared at Joe.

"It must be Moss Murphy."

"Why do you say that?"

"Think about it. I hurt his son, his flesh and blood. Maybe he wants to pay me back in kind."

"If that's true, the man has lost it. If you don't kill him, I'll kill him for sending people into my home."

"I'll kill him, all right, but I'll want to know that he was behind the break-in before I do it. I need to find the people who did the break-in."

"I've got Finn Kelly looking into it. He should be here any minute," Pullo said.

Tanner nodded toward the one-way mirror that looked out over the club.

"There's Kelly now."

Finn Kelly entered the club and paused to speak to the twin bouncers at the door, Michael and Robert. Tanner took note that Kelly had a large envelope tucked under an arm. A short time later, Kelly knocked on the office door and was told to enter by Pullo. Kelly sent Tanner a nod and settled on a stool beside Pullo.

"I have something, Joe, but it's not much. At least not yet."

Kelly opened the envelope and removed a set of photographs. The photos showed a man and a woman, both in their forties and dressed in black. The pictures had been filmed through glass.

"They look familiar, Tanner?"

"No, Joe. I've never seen either of them before."

"Where did you get these, Finn?" Pullo asked.

"From a travel agency a few blocks away. They were taken shortly before the break-in. The couple was picked up on a few other store security cameras, but in those they were just passing by while walking toward your residence."

"Good work, Finn," Pullo said.

Tanner agreed as he studied a photo.

"I know someone who might be able to identify them for us," Tanner said, while thinking of Thomas Lawson. "He's a man with government resources."

Tanner stared at the faces of Michael and Kate Barlow.

Who are you?

7

SPIES FOR HIRE

DETROIT 1994

AT THE AGE OF TWENTY-TWO, the young man who would later go by the name of Michael Barlow was starting at the bottom of the ladder.

Barlow, whose real name was Dennis Polanski, was working in the mail room of one of Detroit's Big Three automakers.

Dennis spent a good chunk of his day roaming the halls in the upper floors of the building. As he worked, he kept his eyes and ears open. A personable young man, Dennis talked sports with the executives and discussed television with their personal assistants.

Dennis had been there for months before he acquired the password that would grant access to the company's research and development department. It was an area that took up three full floors.

Although he worked for one auto company in the mail

room, Dennis was actually employed by an overseas rival to act as an industrial spy.

He'd been approached while still a senior at Wayne State University. His recruiter was a woman in her forties who told him to call her Sue. Sue was Asian, but spoke English with a German accent. Dennis was never certain just what foreign car manufacturer Sue was affiliated with, if any, nor did he care.

Sue gave him a thousand dollars just to hear her out and Dennis was more than happy to listen to her. His father had recently passed away after injuries received in an auto accident. Dennis had been driving at the time, when a drunk ran a red light and T-boned his car. He also had a mother suffering from emphysema, and with his father dead and no money coming in, the medical bills were piling up.

If Sue knew of a way he could bring in serious money to ease his mother's worries, Dennis was willing to break the rules and become a corporate spy.

He received two-hundred a week from Sue, with the promise of ten-thousand dollars if he discovered a way to get into the R&D section of the auto company he worked for. It took several months, but Dennis finally spotted an opportunity.

There was a new executive taking over the research and development section. An electronic swipe card had come in for the new man and Dennis had delivered it to the office the executive would be using. Dennis knew that it was still sitting on the desk inside an envelope. The swipe card combined with the password were all one needed to enter the most sensitive areas of the company.

Sue's people had to get past the security guard and the cameras, but once they grabbed that card from the envelope they could use it to gain entry to the R&D labs.

Dennis had once asked Sue how she would get past

security. She assured Dennis that those issues could be handled with a healthy bribe to the right individuals. After all, Sue reminded him, the guards made the same pittance that he did down in the mail room.

Dennis might have been a lowly mail room worker, but he had no intention of staying one. He was also smarter than Sue realized.

∾

DENNIS' girlfriend, a young lady named Cynthia, looked at him with a shocked expression.

They were in her bed together in the early evening, inside the apartment Cynthia shared with her mother. Her mother worked second shift as an assistant manager of a bar.

Dennis had just confessed to Cynthia that he was actually a corporate spy. He also let her know he was on the cusp of getting a big payoff.

"You're talking about committing a burglary?"

"No, I'm talking about stealing. It will only be classified as a burglary if I get caught by the cops."

Cynthia looked at Dennis as if she were seeing him through new eyes.

"You're brave."

"More than you know. I'm not going to tell Sue about this. I want to get inside the R&D department myself."

"Why take the risk?"

"Money. If I film inside the department I'll have a video worth a whole lot more than ten grand. Cindy, we'll be able to name our own price."

"*Our* own price?"

"I need your help."

"What can I do?"

"The cameras and the swipe card system are all run by

computers. You know all about that stuff. I bet it would be easy for you to shut down the computers and erase my swipes."

"Do they have a back-up generator?"

"Several of them, but the one that backs-up the cameras is broken. The new generator is sitting in a crate on the loading dock. They're planning to install it over Christmas break."

Cynthia stared at Dennis.

"What if I say no?"

"I can't do it without you, so I'll just settle for the ten grand."

Cynthia rose from the bed and slipped into a robe. After pacing a bit, she spoke.

"Are their computers connected to the web?"

"Yeah, even the one in the mail room."

"Could you sneak us into the mail room after it's closed for the day?"

Dennis thought for a moment, then nodded.

"There's a camera aimed at the loading dock door, but I could sneak us in through a window in the bathroom."

"We'd have to do this at night. Better yet, early morning."

Dennis sprang from the bed and grabbed his jeans from the floor. After he slipped into them, he hugged Cynthia.

"You can back out of this at any point, but if we're doing this, we should do it tomorrow night."

"I won't back out. Besides, you'll be the one taking the risk. No one will check the mail room, but I bet they send someone upstairs to look around."

"I know a dozen places to hide, and I'll be quick. If you can kill the cameras for ten minutes they'll never know we were there."

DENNIS' plan went off without a problem, and was even helped by a thunderstorm that caused the lights to flicker. Cynthia hacked into the security computer through the terminal in the mail room and then erased her tracks.

Sue was impressed by Dennis' initiative in getting inside R&D by himself. He never mentioned that he had help from Cynthia. Sue didn't need to know that, and Cynthia didn't need another person aware that she was involved.

Dennis had been prepared to ask Sue for fifty-thousand dollars for his film showing the latest prototypes of her competitor's upcoming vehicles, as well as the notes, scribbles, and equations he had captured on a massive blackboard.

Instead, he asked Sue for a quarter of a million dollars. She paid it gratefully. While his film had value, it was nothing compared to the other information he had obtained. While Dennis was filming the R&D department, Cynthia had been copying files from the computers. Dennis was floored by Cynthia's audacity and amused by the thrill she received from behaving like a bad girl.

Dennis kept working in the mail room until Cynthia finished school. They had hidden most of the money away and continued to live as they had. If Dennis was ever suspected of spying, he was unaware of it.

On the night of her graduation, Dennis proposed to Cynthia.

"We make a good team," Dennis told her, as he opened a box and showed her the engagement ring he'd bought for her. "Marry me?"

Cynthia agreed. When they returned from their Hawaiian honeymoon, Sue introduced Dennis to a friend of hers who was an executive in the pharmaceutical industry.

Both Cynthia and Dennis became employees of the man's main rival. Dennis was once again in the mail room, while

Cynthia was able to land a nice position in the company's expanding data center.

Over the years, Dennis and Cynthia had increased their skill sets and went beyond corporate espionage.

They've worked for many people under various names, with their current identities being those of Michael and Kate Barlow.

They had failed more than once, but had many more successes. They had never been captured, arrested, or suffered more than casual questioning from the authorities or private security. They were professionals of the highest caliber in a field that had few participants.

That definition also applied to Tanner, and Michael and Kate Barlow were now on his radar.

8
DOWN MEXICO WAY

THE BARLOWS CLIMBED INTO THE REAR OF A CHAUFFEUR driven Mercedes and were greeted with a smile by the man who had hired them, Trevor Healy.

Trevor Healy was thirty-four and a former member of The Conglomerate. He had joined Hexalcorp only weeks before they spun off their black ops division and renamed it Ordnance Inc.

Healy was six-foot-two, built thin, and spoke with a New England accent. A handsome man, he had wavy brown hair and green eyes. As one of only six coordinators in Ordnance Inc.'s organization, he wielded great power, but was also to blame whenever anything went wrong.

Trevor's vehicle was parked outside a trendy restaurant on Boca Chica Boulevard in Brownsville, Texas. He was to meet a new client. He hoped the man would be easier to deal with than his current client.

"First, Kate, Michael, let me say that I'm pleased with the progress you two have made, however, the client is getting restless."

"We have an update that may soothe him," Michael said.

"Not only is there a possibility that Marian Parker is still alive, but she may also have had a fourth child. If true, Tanner has a sibling."

Trevor took out his phone. "I'm going to get the client on speakerphone so you two can tell him what you know." Trevor made the call. It was answered by a gruff voice.

"I hope this is good news, Healy."

"It's good news, but not great. While we're fairly certain that Tanner has family, we've yet to find them."

A sigh came over the phone.

"You told me that you hired the best people around. What's taking them so long?"

Michael and Kate exchanged glances with Healy. Their expressions let him know they thought the client was an asshole. If digging into Tanner's life and past was easy, why didn't the client do the deed himself?

"I expect progress will be made very soon, sir," Healy said.

"Maybe I should just send a phony to that ranch and have him claim to be a Parker."

"I would advise against doing that. If Tanner grew suspicious, he would be alerted to your plans for him."

"I guess," said the client. "But I want to speed things up. Tell your people that I'll give them an additional ten thousand dollars if they get me a name and address by tomorrow."

"Tomorrow? Sir, I'm not sure that's a possibility."

"Tomorrow, Healy, or I'll hire someone else."

Trevor Healy gave his phone a disgusted look. Hire someone else? Like whom? A private security company would never have entertained the client's request.

Ordnance Inc. was the only organization offering such services. The client knew that. Still the ill-tempered bastard was the client, as such, he was entitled to have his ass kissed. When Healy spoke again, his voice was respectful.

"I'll call you back tomorrow with a name."

"Do that, Healy."

There was the sound of static as the call ended. Trevor put his phone away and looked at Michael and Kate.

"I'll add another ten thousand to the client's bonus but I need a name by tomorrow night."

"We'd love to claim those bonuses, Trevor," Kate said. "But another day simply might not be enough time. We promise results, not results by a given date."

Michael's head snapped up as an idea occurred to him.

"The woman in Mexico. It's possible that she could lead us right to Tanner's family."

"You're right," Trevor said. "I've hired a team of mercenaries down there to grab her. Once they do, they'll learn everything she knows."

"How soon will they act?"

Trevor checked his watch.

"As a matter of fact, they should be abducting her at any moment."

～

EL RANCHO DE ARMAS AFILADAS, MEXICO, 9:25 p.m.

ALEXA LUCIA PULLED up to the entrance of her ranch and found an unmarked van blocking the driveway. The van looked old and was skewed on an angle. Alexa assumed the vehicle had broken down. She assumed that, but didn't rely on it.

Although she lived in a safe, bucolic area, Alexa knew that you could take nothing for granted. She took out her phone to call the ranch house and a blur of movement came from her left.

Alexa dropped her phone as a crowbar shattered her side window. Bits of glass fell across her legs. That was followed by a hand reaching inside the car and gripping her hair. Alexa opened her door and shoved it into her attacker, who was joined by another man.

Inside the van, a third man brought the vehicle to life and drove it closer. The first two men had each grabbed onto one of Alexa's arms and were dragging her toward the van. They were big men wearing bandanas over their lower faces. Their grips were as tight as a vise.

With her arms supported by the men, Alexa swung her legs up and slammed a knee into the face of the man on her left. The man cried out, his grip slackened, and when a second blow caught him in the throat, he released Alexa.

Alexa reached for one of the knives she kept sheathed in her boots, once she'd freed it, she jammed its blade into the eye of the man who still held her. His scream filled the night, as the other man recovered from the blows he'd received.

Enraged, the man reached for the gun tucked away at the small of his back. He never got to use it, as Alexa freed a second knife from her other boot and sent it on an unerring path. The blade hit the man's Adam's apple as if it were the bullseye on a target. He dropped his gun and wrapped his hands around the knife's handle, as his eyes bulged and his knees gave way.

Alexa went for the man's gun, but heard the sound of a shotgun racking a shell. She looked up as her hand hovered above the gun and saw that the man inside the van was leveling a shotgun at her.

The man was opening his mouth to speak when a shot rang out, and an exit wound appeared above the bridge of his nose, causing a huge bloody hole to form on his forehead.

The shot had been fired from the driveway, where Deke Mercer stood with a rifle pressed to his shoulder.

"Alexa?"

"I'm good, Deke, thanks to you."

Deke came around the van and saw the first two men. Both were writhing in agony from the knives embedded in them. The man with the knife in his throat was losing blood at a steady pace. Deke left him where he lay and moved toward the man with the blade in his eye.

As Deke approached him, the man fumbled at a holster on his hip while cursing his clumsiness. His movements were like those of a drunk. The agony caused by the knife in his skull was more than his brain could deal with. Deke disarmed him as he spoke to the man in Spanish.

"Tell us why you're here and I'll get you to a doctor."

The man answered through slobbering lips.

"We were hired by an American… no name."

"Why?"

"To question the woman about a man named Cody Parker."

Deke turned and looked at Alexa. "This is about Tanner." After seeing her shocked expression, Deke asked the man more questions.

"What is it you were to find out?"

"They want to know if Parker has close family somewhere."

"How do you contact your employer?"

"Phone… inside the van. Now, doctor, please?"

Alexa walked over.

"Do you think he can tell us anything else, Deke?"

"No."

Alexa fired a shot into the man's chest.

"The other one died. Help me get these bodies in the van, then we'll have to find a place to leave them."

"I'll take care of it. You should rest."

"I'm not an invalid. I'll help you."

Deke kissed her, and as he did, he laid a gentle hand on her stomach.

"The baby is kicking."

Alexa smiled.

"She likes the excitement."

9

A BLAST FROM THE PAST

TANNER RETURNED HOME FROM SEEING PULLO AT JOHNNY R'S and found Sara standing by the elevator waiting to greet him.

Sara was on the phone. Whoever she was speaking to, she didn't seem very happy to be hearing from them.

"He's just arrived back," Sara said. That was followed by a pause, then the words, "Yes, and you take care as well."

Sara thrust the phone at Tanner as a tight smile came on her face.

"It's Alexa."

After taking the phone from her, Tanner watched as Sara walked away to give him privacy.

"Alexa? Is everything all right?"

"No. I was attacked by three men tonight. They were sent here by someone who wanted them to interrogate me in order to learn more about you."

"I'm sorry. Were you hurt?"

"No, and it's not your fault, but you should know that someone is trying to find out if you have family out there somewhere."

"I just became aware of this tonight."

"Tanner?"

"Yeah?"

"Cody, they know who you are. They already know you're Cody Parker."

"They said that?"

"Yes, but if they know that, then they must know that you couldn't have any family left. I don't understand why they would still be looking."

"I don't either, and Alexa, thanks for calling. I'm sorry that any of this touched you. I know you don't need that."

"You're with Sara now," Alexa said, as a statement and not a question.

"Yes."

"I think maybe I'm glad about that… maybe."

"And you're with Deke."

"We're married, Tanner."

"I hope you're happy, Alexa."

"I am, and you?"

"I'm good."

"Watch your back, Cody. Someone wants to jam a knife in it."

"Take care, Alexa."

The call ended. Tanner walked into the living room to find Sara pretending to read a magazine. After he explained the reason for Alexa's call, Sara grew worried.

"What if they go after Romeo next?"

"I'll warn him to be careful, but I don't think this is about friends, no matter how close I am to them. Someone out there wants to hit me where it hurts. They want blood of my blood, an eye for an eye."

"You know who's behind this?"

"I suspect it's Moss Murphy attempting to pay me back for hurting his son."

"If so, he's a fool. He's lucky you didn't kill his son for going after you and Joe."

Tanner walked over to the window and took in the magnificent view of the Manhattan skyline. However, he barely noticed it, as his attention was directed inward. After several moments passed, he told Sara he'd be right back, then walked into the home office they had set up. After removing a phone from a desk, he went back into the living room.

"Who are you calling?" Sara asked.

Tanner smiled.

"You might say that I'm calling home."

"You're calling Spenser?"

"No, Stark, Texas."

"Oh, the ranch you grew up on. What's the name of the woman who owns it?"

"Maria Reyes," Tanner said, as he pushed the call button on the phone.

～

THE REYES HORSE RANCH, STARK, TEXAS

GRAHAM RICHARDS, a former physician who went by the name Doc, answered the land line inside the Reyes' ranch house.

"Reyes residence, this is Doc speaking."

"Doc, it's Tanner. Do you remember me?"

"Ha! You're a hard one to forget, son. How're you doing, boy?"

"I'm good, how about you?"

"I've got a roof over my head, food to eat, and a job. That's more than many can say these days."

"Is Maria there?"

"No, that man of hers took her off to Europe. I think he's opening an office in London."

"And what about her children, Javier and Romina?"

"Well, the college thing didn't work out for Javier, but then the boy joined the navy and found his place in the world. Romina's off to college though, out in California."

"Does that mean you're running the ranch?"

"What's left of it. There's been an awful drought around these parts. Maria sold most of the horses before she left for London. You might say I'm more like a caretaker now. Even that may not last. I think she might sell the place."

"She said that?"

"Not in so many words, but once she marries Chuck Willis, they'll probably move to London."

The news that the ranch might be sold hit Tanner harder than he would have imagined. That land had been in his family for generations. There was a part of him that would always be a rancher's son.

He stirred himself from introspection and got to the purpose for his call.

"Doc, has there been any trouble at the ranch?"

"Trouble? No, but something weird happened."

"What's that?"

"Well, you remember that graveyard that belonged to the Parker family, the folks who used to own the ranch?"

"I remember it."

"Somebody tore hell out of it. I reported it to the police, but they didn't know what to make of it."

"The graves were desecrated?" Tanner asked in a whisper.

"It's worse than that. The sick bastards stole two of the bodies, Cody Parker and his mother are missing. If you ask me, it's some kind of Devil worship thing."

Tanner spoke with Doc a few moments more before

ending the call. Sara was at his side, looking troubled by what she had heard of the conversation on Tanner's end.

"Someone violated your family's graveyard?"

Tanner nodded as his face reddened. He told Sara what he had learned from Joe Pullo and that Joe's home had been robbed.

"They only took one thing, a picture of me as a boy that Laurel had. It was a photo of me and my mother."

"And those are the same two graves that had the bodies removed?"

"Yes."

"What's your next move?"

"Joe will be working to find the man and woman who broke into his place. I'll go after it from a different direction."

"Let me help?"

Tanner caressed Sara's cheek.

"Pack a bag. We're going to Texas."

10

GOING HOME

Inside Joe Pullo's office at Johnny R's strip club, Joe discussed business with his Street Boss and Underboss, respectively, Bosco and Finn Kelly. Bosco also acted as Joe's Consigliere, and his advice was sought often by Joe.

As he offered his opinion on the matter of tracking down the people who broke into Pullo's home, Bosco gestured at Kelly.

"Finn will track them down, but he'll need the time to find them."

"You're willing to take on his work for a while?"

"Finn has tracked people down before. Me? I wouldn't know where to start."

Joe tapped his fingers on the edge of his desk as he looked down at the photos of Kate and Michael Barlow that Finn Kelly had uncovered.

"I want these two, Finn, this man and woman. If word got around that I was easy to steal from business would suffer."

"I agree," Finn said. "I'll do my best to find them."

Pullo picked up the photos and stared at them.

"Whoever they are, they've got guts."

73

"May I make a suggestion?" Finn asked.

"I'm always open to good ideas."

"Once I find them, let's leave them alive. People like this could be useful buggers."

Joe stared at Kelly, then glanced over at Bosco.

"He's right," Bosco said. "I can think of a few ways to use their talents. Besides, unless they were stupid enough to go around bragging about it, no one knows they robbed you."

"I'll consider it," Pullo said. "But first we need to find them. Maybe Tanner's government type will be able to help."

"When will we know if he comes up with anything?" Finn asked.

"Tomorrow," Joe said.

~

AFTER TANNER CONTACTED HIM, Thomas Lawson arranged for a private jet to take Tanner and Sara to Texas. They boarded the jet before noon the next day.

As they flew, Tanner spoke to Sara about the Reyes Ranch and the time he'd spent there. He had told her about it before, but not in any detail.

"That was after you leapt onto that train in Ridge Creek?"

"Yeah, with one of your bullets in me."

Sara winced at the memory.

"That seems like a lifetime ago."

When he finished telling the story, Sara was staring at him.

"What?"

"That childhood friend of your sisters, Tonya Jennings? What does she look like?"

"She's beautiful."

"Um-hmm," Sara said. "Perhaps we'll skip seeing her this visit."

Tanner laughed as Sara smiled.

"I like it when you're jealous, but if I ever want anyone else I'll let you know."

Sara leaned over and gave Tanner a long passionate kiss.

"You won't want anyone else."

Tanner took her hand in his.

"Whoever is behind digging up the graves has gone to a lot of trouble. It makes me wonder if they know something that I don't."

"Like what?"

"Maybe I have a sibling that was the product of an affair and put up for adoption."

"If true, it's more likely that your father would have had the affair. A woman would have a harder time concealing a pregnancy."

"Yeah, but it feels odd to think I might have family out there somewhere."

"Is there anyone you could ask about it?"

"There are two people. Doc is one of them. He was our family physician until he crawled into a bottle. He delivered me and my sisters. It's possible he might know everything."

"You said there were two people. Who is the other one?"

"A woman named Emily Sounder. She was my mother's best friend, but I'm not sure she's still alive. If there was an affair that produced a child, Mrs. Sounder would know about it."

"If your father had another son, I wonder if he looks like you."

Sara felt Tanner's grip grow firmer as they held hands.

"What is it? Did you remember something?"

"It's what you said about my father having another son. It stirred a recent memory, but no, it must have been just a coincidence."

"What about your cousin? Has anyone come after him?"

"I called White. He's had no trouble. It's also not common knowledge that we're related since he grew up under an assumed name. The thing is, this is personal. Whoever is looking to hurt me will want a closer relative than a cousin. They likely won't settle for anything less than a sibling or a parent."

"Neither of which you have."

"As far as I know."

Their jet landed and Tanner was pleased to see that Lawson had arranged for a rental car. Tanner gathered their luggage and headed off toward the Reyes Ranch.

For only the second time in twenty years, he was going home.

11

HE AIN'T HEAVY

AT THE REYES RANCH, DOC HAD RISEN EARLY AND TENDED TO the few horses that remained on the property. After feeding the chickens and taking care of a few other chores, he climbed into an all-terrain vehicle and went out to check the fences.

As a precaution, Doc always took along a rifle in case he ran across a predator that might go after the chickens, along with the occasional roof rat.

On this day, he suspected that he had run across vermin of a different kind. He spotted a man standing near the graves of the Parker family.

The young man looked up as Doc approached, alerted by the sound of the all-terrain vehicle. Doc kept the rifle ready to grab as he spoke to the man.

"You're on private property, son."

The man pointed at the graves. When he spoke, Doc knew he wasn't from the area.

"Do the police know what happened here yet? Who it was that did this?"

"No names, but they must be some major league assholes to go around defiling graves."

"Two of the graves are empty."

"The bodies were stolen, and Lord only knows why."

The young man scowled.

"Are you Reyes?"

"No, but I work for Mrs. Reyes. My name's Doc."

"I don't mean to trespass. I just came to see the graves. These people... they were my family."

Doc shook his head.

"I heard the Parkers had no family left."

The man smiled.

"I could tell you my story over a cup of coffee."

Doc laughed.

"Climb on in, son. I was just about to scramble some eggs back at the house, and the coffee is already brewed."

The man took a seat in the ATV and Doc asked him his name.

"Parker, I'm Caleb Parker."

$\sim$

MICHAEL BARLOW WAS LATHERED with soap inside the shower of a Brownsville, Texas hotel suite when he heard his wife cry out.

He rushed from the shower and nearly slipped and fell as he ran down the short hallway to the living area.

"Cindy, are you all right?"

His wife smiled as she took in his soapy nakedness, then reprimanded him.

"I'm Kate Barlow, remember? If you slip up and use my real name around the wrong people we'll be in big trouble."

"I thought you were in trouble. I heard you scream."

Kate looked at his crotch.

"Is that the only weapon you brought with you?"

Michael grabbed a T-shirt and used it to wipe off the soap he wore.

"I wasn't thinking. I just wanted to get to you and help you."

"That's sweet, baby, but I didn't scream, I cheered."

"Cheered?"

"Cody Parker has a brother. I just found him."

"How?"

"I finally looked in the right place. Marian Parker used her maiden name. A Marian Gant is listed as the mother of a boy whose father was named Frank Parker, the right Frank Parker, not the endless other Frank Parkers we've run across. Damn Tanner for having such a common surname."

"How do we locate Tanner's brother?"

Kate grinned.

"Get this, the man is here in Texas. I hacked into the system and accessed his credit card. His plane landed early this morning."

Michael rushed to his wife and scooped her up out of the chair she sat in.

Kate laughed as Michael carried her toward the bedroom.

"What are you doing?"

Michael laid her atop the bed and began unbuttoning her blouse.

"I want to celebrate the fact that my wife is a genius."

"By boffing me?"

"I'll use any excuse, you know that."

Kate shed her clothes and the two of them crawled beneath the covers.

"That bonus is ours, baby," Kate said.

"And soon we'll be on a plane for Rio," Michael said, as his hands explored Kate's body.

∿

In the afternoon, Doc greeted Tanner with a handshake while sending Sara a warm smile.

On the ride in from the airport, Tanner and Sara saw firsthand the effects of the prolonged drought that the area had suffered through.

That drought had been followed by a devastating hurricane, although the Stark area saw little damage caused by wind or flooding.

There were the remains of blackened trees from fires, and creeks that were either dry or far below their usual levels. The fields, which under normal conditions were still green, had turned brown and were dotted by weeds. A foreclosure sign hung on a property bordering the ranch, and Tanner knew that Stark, Texas had fallen on hard times.

"I called Maria," Doc said. "She was sorry she wouldn't be here to see you. She also asked me to offer you the guest room."

"Next time you talk to her, tell her I said thanks, but we have a reservation for a hotel room."

Doc looked at the two of them.

"Why are you here, son?"

"I've come to solve a mystery. I'd also like to get a look at those graves again."

"You aren't the only one. People from town have been coming out here to see what happened. Some of them are even bringing up those ghost stories that Romina told us about."

"She did say something about people seeing ghosts out there. What was it?"

"One of the veterinarians who isn't around anymore swore he saw Marian Parker out at the graves once, and several people have claimed to have seen Cody or Frank Parker."

"What about you? Have you ever seen anything?"

Doc considered telling Tanner about the young man claiming to be one of the Parker family. However, the man had asked Doc to keep his existence to himself. He had told Doc that he only came to pay his respects after reading an article about the graves being disturbed. He just wanted to mourn his family in peace. Doc decided to respect the young man's wishes and not tell anyone about him.

"No, Tanner. I've never seen anything strange out there. I can't say that I believe in ghosts either."

∼

TANNER AND SARA walked across the dry earth to the spot where the Parker family was buried.

When Tanner looked down inside the empty grave that bore his name, it made his earlier life as Cody Parker seem almost like a dream.

Then, he looked into the hole that had once held his mother, along with the disturbed graves of his other family members. Anger welled up inside him and demanded an outlet, but as yet, he had no one to vent it on. Whoever was responsible for committing these atrocities would pay. If it was Moss Murphy, as Tanner suspected, he would hunt the man down and kill him.

"What sort of person robs a grave?" Sara said with disgust.

Tanner felt his phone vibrate. It was Thomas Lawson with news.

Lawson was aware that Tanner's mother bore the maiden name of Gant. He learned that fact when Tanner discovered that he was the cousin of Jessica White's husband. After being made aware that a photo of Marian Gant existed, Lawson had the picture scanned and sent through a search program equipped with facial recognition software.

"We had one hit. The photo was found inside the wreckage of a motor home that once belonged to Jeffrey Mitchell, the serial killer. It was assumed that she was a possible victim of Mitchell's, but now it looks like it was left there when White's father, your late uncle, used the trailer."

"Can you send me the photo?"

"Yes, but I wanted to warn you first. The photo was singed from the fire that consumed the motor home. The bottom right corner is missing, but the people in the photo are clear."

"How many people were with my mother?"

"Only one, a young boy, and Tanner, the facial recognition software placed your mother's age between thirty-two and thirty-five."

"My mother died when she was twenty-nine... or so I was told."

"The boy in the picture was three. There's an inscription on the back of the photo that states his age. I'll send you copies of both the front and the rear of the photo."

"Thank you, Lawson. I'm going to owe you one after this."

"I'm glad I can help. And Tanner, watch your back."

Tanner ended the call and explained the situation to Sara. When the photo came through on the phone, Tanner was amazed. He had been expecting to see a blurred snapshot that was decades old, instead, he saw a photo that captured his mother as he remembered her.

"She was beautiful, Tanner, and you have her eyes," Sara said. "But does the little boy look familiar at all?"

"Yes, he looks like my father."

A second file arrived. This one displayed the rear of the photo and the inscription it bore. The words had been written in pen, likely by Tanner's mother. When he read them, an uncharacteristic chill went down Tanner's spine.

ME AND CALEB ON HIS THIRD BIRTHDAY.

Tanner touched the screen of his phone as he traced a finger across the faces.

"A brother. I have a brother."

12

THE CLIENT

K<small>ATE</small> B<small>ARLOW HEARD RELIEF IN</small> T<small>REVOR</small> H<small>EALY'S VOICE AFTER</small> she gave him the name of Tanner's brother, but she was surprised by Healy's laughter when she informed him that the man was in Texas.

"Oh, the client will love that. What name is the man using?"

Kate gave him the name, along with more news.

"He was adopted?"

"Yeah, and he didn't grow up in Texas. He grew up in—oh hold on a second and let me grab my notes."

Kate gave Healy all of the information she had on Tanner's brother. With that done, she informed him she was placing the call on speakerphone so that her husband could talk to Healy too.

"We've delivered, Healy. I expect our bonuses and our fee to be deposited into the accounts we set up."

"That's going to have to wait until we have DNA verification; but don't worry, Michael, you'll get paid."

"Bullshit! The client won't wait for DNA tests and neither

85

will we. We've completed the job and now we want to get paid."

"That's not how it works, Michael. You know that. We've worked together before."

"I don't care how it works. We want the money today."

Healy could be heard exhaling loudly on the line before he spoke again.

"What's going on, guys? Why the hurry to get paid?"

There was silence, but then Kate spoke.

"It's Tanner, Trevor. We've researched this man thoroughly. If he ever connects us to what's been going on we're as good as dead. Michael and I want to get away as soon as we can."

"The client will handle Tanner. He'll be dead any day now."

"Maybe, but I don't think so. If even a fraction of the stories and myths about the man are true, he's an unstoppable killing machine."

"Let's say you're right. He's still just a guy with a gun. He's not a P.I. or a bounty hunter. He'll have no clue how to find any of us. Listen, I'll deposit the bonuses, but you'll have to wait for the fee. That's fair, right?"

Michael grumbled, but then said, "Yeah, we'll take that. I guess you're right. A guy like Tanner wouldn't possess the skills to find us. Deposit the bonuses. Kate and I are leaving here soon."

～

SARA HAD SPENT a great deal of the flight to Texas on the phone.

She had been calling home improvement stores in the area where the town of Stark was located while asking the clerks if anyone had recently purchased a large supply of shovels and pickaxes. The clerk at a hardware store in Bando said he remembered selling such equipment.

"Oh yeah, they took everything we had in the store, along with work gloves and headlamps. That was the best day we've had since that damn megastore opened up last year."

Sara relayed the information to Tanner and told him that Lawson might be able to figure out who bought the shovels. With any luck, it was the same people who dug up the graves.

Tanner was about to call Lawson when he had a better idea.

"I know someone else who could help, and I owe them a call."

～

"TANNER? How are you? Hey, Madison, Tanner's on the line."

Tanner smiled as he heard the genuine pleasure in Tim Jackson's voice. There weren't many people who delighted in getting a call from Tanner, but Tim was one of them.

Tanner had saved Tim and Madison Jackson from trouble, the type of trouble that can make you dead. Tim Jackson, a world-class hacker, was always ready to help Tanner if needed.

After introducing Sara on the line, and saying hello to Madison, Tanner got to the purpose for his call.

"Give me an hour and I'll have the guy's shoe size," Tim said.

～

AFTER TALKING to Michael and Kate Barlow, Trevor Healy arranged to meet with the client.

Trevor was preoccupied with thoughts of another operation that was beginning. The target of that assignment was the husband of Dr. Jessica White, the famed criminal profiler. Trevor was unaware that White and Tanner were cousins, but was cognizant of the fact that Mr. White was a dangerous man to cross.

The operation against White required much planning and coordination. It was to be placed in action the next day. Trevor was hoping to finish with Tanner as soon as possible, to free up his time.

The client arrived in a rented limousine but had one of his own men driving the car. There was also a bodyguard, an incredibly tall and massive young man with red hair who must have filled half the limo. Healy had heard the man referred to as the Irish Hulk.

A handsome man with graying dark hair stepped out of the limo with a cigar in his hand. There were rings under his eyes and he looked haggard, as if he weren't getting enough sleep. His name was Moss Murphy.

Trevor knew Murphy hated Tanner. Hated the man enough to launch an investigation into his past, hated him enough to leave Boston and travel to Texas, so that he could torture the man himself.

Tanner had harmed Murphy's son, Liam Murphy, and the elder Murphy wanted vengeance more than he wanted to breathe.

"You have a photo?"

"My people obtained one by hacking into the DMV," Trevor said as he handed Murphy a file.

Murphy studied the photo and made a face.

"He doesn't look like Tanner."

"Turn to page four. There you'll find photos of Tanner's father and mother."

Murphy did as Trevor suggested, then smiled.

"Yeah, the kid looks like the father, but Tanner got them eyes from his mother. And what about her? Where is she?"

"That's still unknown. If she's not dead, then she's dropped off the face of the earth."

"It doesn't matter. Tanner's brother will be enough. Good work, Healy."

"Thank you, sir. Can we expect payment later today?"

"Hell no. I want DNA confirmation."

"That takes time. I thought you would move on Tanner quickly."

"Oh, I'll kill the guy we believe is Tanner's brother. If the DNA tests later prove he's not, then so what? All we've lost is a little time. But no, this guy is Tanner's brother. By tomorrow, I'll have made that prick Tanner suffer."

"About that, I have a Hammer Team standing by in case it becomes necessary to control Tanner by other means. The threat of having his brother murdered might not be enough to bring him to his knees."

"A Hammer Team? It sounds expensive."

"They are, but they'll kill Tanner if nothing else works." Trevor took out his phone. "I need to check on the man I have in place. If he gives us the okay, the plan can go into effect now."

"You've already grabbed Tanner's Brother?"

"No, but he checked into a motel in Stark, near the ranch. We can grab him at any time."

Trevor made the call, but received disappointing news, which he passed on to Murphy.

"The timing isn't right yet, but when it is, we'll shut the trap and make Tanner suffer."

Murphy grinned.

"Don't worry about that. I've got my own guys coming in, along with a group of mercenaries. I plan to set a trap for Tanner, and his brother will be the bait."

～

"YOU'RE the second person today to ask me about that."

Finn Murphy leaned on the scarred counter of a hardware store located near Stark, Texas. Like Sara, Finn had the idea to trace the grave robbers. He didn't care about them, but he hoped they would lead him to Michael and Kate Barlow, the people who broke into Joe Pullo's home.

The clerk was in his thirties and had thinning brown hair. A name tag was pinned to his red and green flannel shirt. It read—My Name is Stan.

"Who asked you before I did?"

"Some woman on the phone. She sounded real cute too."

"Did she say why she was asking?"

"No, and say, what kind of accent you got?"

"I'm from Ireland."

"Get out of here. My wife is Irish. Her maiden name is O'Leary."

"All the O'Leary's I know are good people," Finn said.

"You haven't met my wife's father."

More conversation with the clerk dislodged a nugget of information. One of the men buying shovels had said something about the town of Stark.

Finn Kelly left the store and drove back to Stark. He had taken a motel room there upon his arrival to Texas.

As he drove along, Finn studied the landscape. There was something familiar about it, the endless vistas, the hills in the distance.

He chalked it up to the fact that he had spent his first few years of life in the state, and in an area that was scant miles from where he was driving.

He'd never settle in Texas. Finn liked cities. Still, there was the feeling of coming home.

13

FAKE BEARD, REAL BLOOD

TIM JACKSON CAME THROUGH FOR TANNER. HE GAVE TANNER the name of the man who had bought the picks and shovels used to unearth Tanner's family. The name was William Price.

"Unfortunately, the name is a phony. I'd bet on it," Tim Jackson said. "The good news is, the man used the same credit card to check into an inn on US77, near a town called Raymondville, Texas."

"I know the area," Tanner said. "It's not far from where I am."

The line grew silent. Tanner waited for the question he knew was coming.

"Um, Tanner… are you going to… I mean, does this guy really have to—"

"This man was involved in the desecration of my family's graves, Tim. I still don't know what happened to two of the bodies."

A gasp came over the line. It was followed by an exclamation.

"Fuck him then! Give me a call if you need anything else."

"Thanks, Tim."

~

TWO HOURS LATER

BILLY PRICE, which was not his real name, smiled beneath the ski mask he wore. He was with three other members of Ordnance Inc. and going by the code-name of Beta. Billy was thirty and had never had a job in his life, at least, not an honest job.

He was of average height, with wide shoulders, a narrow waist, and a pleasant face.

Working for Ordnance Inc. was the best gig he'd ever had. The money was steady and large.

Of course, you had to have the stomach for the work. Billy had the stomach. He had been committing heinous acts since he was in grade school.

He knew if he kept his head down and continued climbing the ladder, he could run the organization someday. He was already tapped to become an Alpha, a team leader. Once he gained that promotion, his income would take a giant leap.

To Billy Price, other people were things. He could mimic their emotions, but with the exception of anger or envy, he felt nothing. That was why he volunteered to be the one to kill the baby.

Ordnance Inc. had been contracted by a client to murder the man's main business rival, along with his young family.

The man had a wife, a two-year-old son, and a six-month-old baby girl. The family had to be killed in such a way that the police would never trace the murders back to

Ordnance Inc.'s client. The only way to ensure that outcome was to leave the cops an easy trail to follow.

Price and the other members of his team had spent the last eight days breaking into area houses and robbing them when the owners weren't home.

They had been destructive. At one home, they fed a water hose inside the house and turned it on. By the time the owners returned from work, the home was flooded. At another house, they set a fire that gutted the structure, while a third home got off easy. At that home, they spray-painted obscene graffiti on the walls and on the furniture.

The vandalism was meant to look like the work of juvenile minds. Price and his friends had a street gang all picked out to take the fall.

Once they killed the target and his family, they would drive a van full of stolen goods to the neighborhood where the street gang lived and leave the keys in it. When a member of the gang took the bait, an anonymous call would come in to the police, and arrests were inevitable.

They had even beat up one of the gang's members and stolen his vest. The vest had the gang's colors and insignia, a red and blue grinning skull. That vest would be found beneath the van's driver's seat, soaked into it would be the blood of the baby girl.

PRICE TOOK out his knife as another of his team, a man using the code-name of Charlie, held the parents at bay. They were in the kitchen of a renovated farm house, where the family had been enjoying dinner.

The mother had freaked out when they broke in the back door. Both she and the husband had been beaten, tied to their chairs, and gagged.

Their little boy was in his highchair. He was crying, but it wasn't loud and whiny, so Price figured the neighbors would never hear it. Besides, the nearest neighbors were a football field away.

The baby was another matter. She had been asleep in a bassinet and, amazingly, had slept through the beatings, but her brother's persistent crying had woken her. In another few seconds, she would be doing her own crying.

Price looked at the open back door and wondered what was taking Alpha and Delta so long. They had grabbed the family's electronics and jewelry to take out to the van. That was over a minute ago. They should have been back inside.

Footsteps came from outside and Price assumed it was one of his two team members returning. When the man with the bandana over his lower face entered the home with a gun, Price dropped his knife and raised his hands in the air.

His partner, Charlie, swung his weapon toward the man. As he did so, the man fired.

There was almost no sound produced as the round left the man's gun. Price wondered what miracle silencer the stranger was using. As for Charlie, he collapsed to the kitchen floor and moaned. Judging by the puddle of blood forming beneath him, Charlie would soon be dead.

The man who shot Charlie spoke to Price. Price was distracted and almost didn't catch what the man was saying. He had been engrossed by staring into the stranger's intense eyes.

"You're coming with me, Price."

"What's this about?"

"Pick up the knife you dropped."

"Why?"

"Pick up the knife and place it in the hand of the man. He should be able to free himself with it, given time."

Price did as he was told, then shrugged.

94

"What now?"

"Start walking or I'll shoot you in the knee and drag you out of here."

Price hesitated, but then he moved. As he was walking toward the door, the baby began to wail.

≈

TO PRICE'S SURPRISE, there was a woman outside. She also had her face covered. She was holding a shotgun and standing over the unconscious forms of Alpha and Delta, who had their wrists and ankles bound by zip ties.

Price was marched to a car that was parked halfway down the home's winding driveway. As he turned to ask the man a question, he was hit on the side of the head.

The lights went out.

≈

TANNER STARED down at Billy Price. Price was sitting on the ground with his back to a tree and his arms tied behind him. His ankles were also bound. He wasn't gagged. There was no need. They were so far out in the desert that no one would hear his screams.

Sara had taken the car to high ground where she could keep watch. Tanner was pleased by that. She didn't need to see what he would do to Billy Price.

A fake beard hung from Price's face. The other men also had beards and Tanner wondered if theirs were fake as well.

Tanner had removed the bandana he'd worn at the house. Billy Price would not be telling anyone what he looked like. Besides, his face was in shadows since the half-lit moon was at his back.

A thin line of dried blood ran down the side of Price's

right cheek. Tanner had struck him at the hairline. Spots of blood marred the black suit Price wore. The other men had worn black suits as well, along with red ties. Tanner wondered if the beards and the suits were a type of disguise, or perhaps a uniform. He had also found a pair of mirrored sunglasses in Price's pocket.

Price moaned, then stirred, and Tanner spoke to him.

"Wake up!"

Price opened his eyes and looked around. When he focused on Tanner, he frowned.

"I'm out in the desert. That's not good."

"You were part of a group that dug up several graves in Stark, Texas. Who hired you?"

"Listen to me. I'm a nobody. It's like you said, I was just part of a group. I don't know who hired us." Price stopped talking and winced. "Damn, my head hurts."

"Why the fake beard?"

"It's how we work. Fake beards, mirrored glasses, black suits, red ties."

"Who's we?"

"Ordnance Inc., I've heard they used to be a part of Hexalcorp."

"Give me the names of the people who helped you with the graves."

"I can't. We use code names like Alpha, Beta, Charlie, Delta. This time out I was named Beta. When we dug up the graves I was Foxtrot."

"Who was in charge?"

"Alpha is always in charge, but there were two other people there. They're the ones you want. They wanted to see what was in the graves."

"Names?"

"Michael and Kate Barlow. They're in their forties, white, dark-haired, and pretty average looking."

Tanner stared at Price.

"Why are you so calm?"

Price shrugged.

"It's how I am."

Tanner understood. Although he wasn't a sociopath like Price, he wasn't easily rattled or distracted by what he might be feeling. When the time came to act, he acted. Emotions and thoughts could be sifted through later.

Tanner raised his gun and pointed it at Price.

"Don't shoot me," Price said.

"Why shouldn't I?"

"Because I'm helping you. I know things too."

"Like what?"

"You're Tanner, right? The hit man?"

Tanner nodded, then said, "Yes," after recalling that Price could barely make him out in the darkness.

"This is about you. I heard Michael Barlow talking about you. He also said that one of the women we dug up was a phony, and that the real one might still be alive. Her name was Marian."

"Do you know where to find her?"

"No, but Michael or Kate Barlow might, and I know where they are."

"Where?"

Price smiled.

"I want to make a deal."

"I could torture the information out of you, Price. You're in no position to deal."

"Hear me out. A dozen of us dug up those graves. The others work together often, but not me. I was brought in to help and to get experience. Ordnance Inc. is grooming me to be an Alpha, a leader. Let me live and I'll find the others and kill them for you."

"You want to kill a dozen people for me?"

"Actually, only ten. The man you shot earlier, Charlie, he's like me, being groomed to be an Alpha. He was one of the grave diggers. And of course, I won't kill myself."

Tanner stared at Price and found himself believing the man was serious.

"How do I know you won't just run?"

"And have to look over my shoulder for you the rest of my days? Hell no. I'd rather kill those people for you and get on with my life. But we have to have a deal."

"Why take my word?"

"What choice do I have, Tanner? Besides, your reputation says you don't fuck around. Your word is probably better than most."

Tanner kept staring at Price. He believed he was telling the truth.

"We have a deal."

"You'll let me live once I kill the others?"

"Yes."

"And healthy, you have to leave me healthy."

Tanner smirked. Price was smart.

"All right. I won't harm you either."

He cut Price free. After peeling off his phony beard, Price stumbled as he rose. He was attempting to stand on feet that had been growing numb.

"Where can I find this Kate and Michael Barlow?"

Price gave Tanner the name of a hotel in Brownsville, Texas.

"I can't promise they're still there, but they were there yesterday."

Tanner pointed his gun at Price.

"If you run I'll track you down and kill you."

"I won't run, and you'll know when I've killed them. I'll make it newsworthy."

"Aren't you worried about Ordnance Inc. coming after you?"

"No. I'll have an alibi, and they've no reason to suspect me anyway. My guess is they won't know what to make of it."

Tanner pointed east.

"You'll find a dirt road three miles that way. Once you reach it, go left and you'll find the highway."

Price frowned.

"I'm a city boy. Are there any predators out here that might get me?"

"Just me, Price. Now start walking."

Tanner watched as Price picked his way along the desert by using the moonlight to see by. When the man was out of sight, Tanner jogged back to where Sara waited for him.

"I didn't hear a shot," she said.

"We made a deal. He kills the other people who desecrated the graves and I let him live."

"Was that his idea?"

"Yeah."

"I'm glad I'm not his friend."

"He doesn't have friends. He wouldn't even understand the concept."

Tanner asked Sara to drive to Brownsville. As they moved along the highway, he sent a text to Tim Jackson about Michael and Kate Barlow. He wanted to know as much about them as they seemed to know about him.

After looking at the clock on the dash, Tanner made a decision.

"Forget Brownsville. We'll stay in Stark. There's someone I need to talk to."

"Who's that?"

"A woman named Emily Sounder. If my mother is still alive, Mrs. Sounder will know."

"You're going to tell her who you are?"

"Yeah, but she'll know. For a while there after our mom died, she was like a second mother to me and my sisters."

"Do you think your mother is alive, Tanner?"

Tanner took out his phone and stared at the picture of his mother and the little boy.

"I don't know, but if she is, she must think I'm dead."

Sara reached over and caressed his cheek.

"You're not dead, Cody Parker. You just might wind up with some family once this mess is settled."

"Family," Tanner said. "A brother, maybe I'll even have my mother back, but Sara, what the hell could have happened to my mother?"

"I don't know, but I'll help you find out."

Tanner turned his head and stared at Sara.

"Thank you."

"Not all family is blood-related, baby."

"I know. Spenser taught me that a long time ago."

14

GHOST TALES

THE FOLLOWING MORNING, TANNER WALKED UP THE WELL-worn steps of Emily Sounder's front porch and rang her doorbell.

Tanner had visited the home many times while growing up. He had fond memories of Mrs. Sounder.

She had been in her fifties the last time he saw her, a robust woman full of energy. Time, as it does with all of us, had aged Emily Sounder and sapped her vitality. The old woman that opened the door looked small, frail, and fearful.

"Yes?"

"Mrs. Sounder. Do you remember me?"

"I don't know you."

Tanner pointed out at the front yard.

"I used to come by and cut your lawn when I was in high school, and when I was a boy you had a cat named Cloud that went up that oak tree. I climbed up there and brought him down. You put bandages on my scratches."

Emily Sounder stared at Tanner, then at the tall tree. He could see her mind working as she recalled the incident. Once she'd remembered it, she shook her head vehemently.

"That was a boy named Cody Parker. He's passed away."

"Look at me, Mrs. Sounder. Look at my eyes. I have my mother's eyes; you always said that."

Mrs. Sounder searched his face as her own displayed her confusion.

"Cody? Are you really Cody?"

"I am, Mrs. Sounder. I survived the massacre and pretended to be dead so that the drug cartel wouldn't kill me."

Emily Sounder stepped out onto the porch. She smiled as she laid a cool, wrinkled hand on Tanner's cheek.

"Oh, Cody. It's a miracle."

"Yes, and I'm hoping for another one."

"You're talking about your mother?"

"I am… and a brother?"

"You know about Caleb?"

"Only recently."

"This has to do with that grave robbing at the ranch?"

"Yes, but Mrs. Sounder, where can I find my mother?"

"Come inside, boy. I've a lot to tell you."

～

"BILLY GANT? MY MOTHER'S BROTHER?"

"Yes. He kidnapped your mother while making it look like she died. DNA testing wasn't common then, and that wreck, that fire… there wasn't much left of the body."

They were seated together in Mrs. Sounder's living room. The furniture was of good quality, but showed signs of wear. Tanner had explained in the most general of terms his survival of the massacre, and Mrs. Sounder didn't press him for details.

"Why would Billy Gant abduct his own sister?"

"Marian told me he was keeping a promise he'd made to

their father, that madman who ran the doomsday cult. Billy swore to bring your mother 'back into the fold' as he put it, and he did so."

"How did you learn all this?"

"Marian told me. She wasn't well when she came to see me, Cody. She never named her illness, but I'm thinking it was cancer. Once she became ill, Billy Gant kicked her and Caleb out of their compound." Mrs. Sounder wiped at tears. "All Marian could think about was coming home to her family… but that was months after the massacre. I think learning that you were all gone nearly killed her outright. If not for Caleb she would have given up."

"Do you know where I can find Caleb?"

"No. He'd be a young man by now, and Cody, he looks like Frank, like your father."

"I never heard it mentioned that my mother was pregnant when the accident happened."

"No one knew. Marian was coming home from the doctor after having a pregnancy test. She was going to surprise your father. After the accident, the doctor and I both kept silent about the pregnancy, as a mercy to your father. It was horrible enough that he lost a wife. He didn't have to know he'd also lost a child."

"I don't understand. Given that she was pregnant, wouldn't that have proven that the body removed from the car wasn't my mother?"

"It would have, but only the doctor and I knew about the pregnancy, and we had no reason to suspect anything. The weather that day was foul, dangerous, and there was a pile-up out on the highway that killed some other folks. Maybe I should have been suspicious, but I certainly wasn't. I was just grieving for the loss of my friend."

"Do you have any idea what could have happened to Caleb?"

"No. I'm so sorry, Cody, but I don't know. Marian stayed here for a day or two, then she was on the move again. I did get the idea that she had a plan. You also need to know something, you're not the first to come looking for her lately."

"The others who came to see you, were they a man and a woman in their forties?"

"Yes, do you know them?"

"No, but I hope to be making their acquaintance soon."

Mrs. Sounder made a face of disapproval.

"I told them nothing. Don't trust them, Cody. They have a quality about them that's hard to explain, but I didn't like either of them."

"The tales about the ghosts seen out at the graves, that began during my mother's visit, didn't it?"

"Yes. Marian went to see the graves with Caleb. Back then, the local teens used the abandoned ranch for a sort of hang-out. One of them must have recognized your mother, and the rumors of ghosts began."

~

As he was leaving her home, Emily Sounder hugged Tanner, but then she stepped back to look at him.

"Tell me something, Cody. Have you had a good life?"

"Yes," Tanner said. "I've had a good life."

"And have you found a good woman?"

"That's a yes, too."

"I'm glad, son. And know this, Cody, your mother loved you more than anything."

"I know she loved me," Tanner said. "She told me so every day of my life."

~

TANNER HAD JUST DRIVEN AWAY from Mrs. Sounder's home when his phone alerted him that he had a text. It was from Thomas Lawson.

He pulled off the road and onto a gravel strip so that he could read the message.

Another picture has been discovered that seems to show the same little boy who was in the photo with your mother. It's a very clear shot, a close-up, and the boy appears to be older. The photo was found inside the trailer of a man named Dave Cully. Cully is deceased, but he was a member of your late uncle's gang.

Tanner downloaded the attachment and stared at the photo. Although the boy in the photo was young, so very young, Tanner was certain he had met the man recently, had met him and felt a connection to him.

After clearing the photo, he searched his memory for a number he'd been given by Joe Pullo. The man on the other end answered after two rings.

"Kelly, here."

"Finn, it's Tanner... there's something I need to tell you."

15

LOVE OR FAMILY?

Sara was in the middle of doing her nails when she heard the sound of dishes clattering. After rising from the sofa, she looked out the peephole in her hotel room door.

She saw a clumsy room service waiter in a white jacket picking up dishes from the hallway floor. She was unable to see his face as he was turned away. She looked back at her own cart. She had only had toast and coffee, but figured she might as well push it out into the hall to be taken away.

Before she could act, another man appeared. He was wearing a suit. He stooped down to lend a hand to the waiter.

"You need to be more careful, Maurice. If you break another dish Kenny will fire you."

"Yes, Mr. Pearson," the other man said.

Sara was about to turn from the scene when the man in the suit stood and knocked on her door.

"Front desk, Mr. Myers. Someone left an envelope for you, sir."

Sara opened the door and saw the bearded man smiling at her. He wore a red tie, and Sara remembered what Tanner had said about Ordnance Inc. members wearing beards, black suits, and red ties. Before she could react, the man sprayed something in her face. The gas was a derivative of Halothane vapor. It was fast-acting and safe, if not used to excess.

Sara wrinkled her nose as if to sneeze, then felt consciousness slipping away.

She crumpled to the floor as her knees collapsed, and fell backwards into the room.

~

OUT IN THE HALLWAY, "MR. PEARSON" continued his act for the benefit of anyone listening behind a closed door.

"You say your faucet is leaking? Maurice, please come in here and take a look at the faucet."

The room service waiter entered with the cart from the hall, then shut and locked the door behind him. After checking Sara to make sure she was out, the man stripped off the white coat he was wearing, only to reveal that he wore another one beneath it.

"Mr. Pearson" put on the removed coat before pointing at the cart that had been pushed into the room.

The other man took his meaning and began opening the cart. It was a phony room service cart that was larger than normal. They would load Sara into it and sneak her out of the hotel.

"Remember, the man watching the cameras has been paid off," Pearson said.

"We still have to deal with the kitchen workers."

"We won't go out through the kitchen. We're leaving through a side door. Relax, everything will go smoothly. Once we hand her over to Murphy's people we're done."

They lifted and loaded Sara into the cart, but then had

trouble shutting it. Pearson saw the problem. It was the heels of her shoes. He stripped the shoes off Sara's feet and tossed them into a corner of the room.

"She won't need shoes. She'll be dead soon."

From inside his jacket, Pearson removed a clear plastic bag that contained a cell phone. There was a yellow note attached to the phone. It was addressed to Tanner.

With Sara concealed inside the cart, a white tablecloth was draped over it. The men pushed the contraption out into the hall and placed the Do Not Disturb sign on the door handle. With that done, they headed for the service elevator.

Back inside the room, Sara's phone began to ring.

~

WHEN SARA HAD FAILED to answer her phone, Tanner assumed she was in the shower or perhaps had stepped out of the room for a moment.

After his second call went unanswered, Tanner rushed back to the hotel.

He found the note, dialed the number on it, and heard the voice of Moss Murphy.

"You messed with the wrong man, Tanner. After what you did to Liam, I can't make you suffer enough."

"Where's Sara?"

"I'll tell you... Cody Parker. I'll also tell you where you can find your asshole brother."

"I don't have a brother, Murphy. My family all died years ago."

"That's bullshit and we both know it; otherwise, why would you be in Stark, Texas?"

"Drop this now, Murphy, and I'll let Liam live. If not, I'll kill both of you."

"You won't find Liam. Even I don't know where Liam is. But wherever he is he's out of your reach."

"Where's Sara?"

"I'll tell you gladly. She's being held out at an old mill off highway 281 in a town called Bando. A few of my guys are with her. They have orders to kill her at noon."

Tanner knew the mill Murphy mentioned. It was a crumbling wooden structure near a narrow stream. He could reach it by car long before noon arrived.

"What's the catch?"

Murphy laughed.

"Oh, did I mention that your brother is in town? He came to Stark on his own for some reason, maybe he read about the graves being disturbed. In any event, he's here, he's being watched, and he's going to die."

Tanner closed his eyes as his hand tightened around the phone.

"You want me to make a choice between Sara and my brother?"

"That's right, and either way you lose."

"Murphy."

"What?"

"I'll find you and I'll kill you."

"Wrong. You'll never leave Texas alive."

"Where's my brother?"

Murphy laughed again.

"We have him at a local motel. My men are watching him. When noon comes, they'll kill him."

"What's the name of the motel?"

"Ah, blood is thicker than water, and I was told that you and Miss Blake were serious."

"The name of the motel, Murphy."

"The Alcott Motel. Don't bother trying to phone and warn him. My men disabled the land line and have signal jammers in place. Look at the time, Tanner. If you don't move soon they'll both die."

Tanner ended the call and rushed from the room. He wasn't headed for the old mill or the Alcott Motel. He had another destination in mind.

He was going to the Reyes Ranch.

16

RIDE 'EM COWBOY!

As he was headed toward the ranch, Tanner received a call from Thomas Lawson.

Tanner's cousin, Mr. White, was having his own problems. Members of Ordnance Inc. were involved.

After Tanner made Lawson aware that Sara had been abducted, Lawson offered to help.

"Thanks, Lawson, but Murphy's people would know a cop or a Fed a mile away, and he must have spotters in place."

"I'll still put a team of Homeland Security agents on standby. Once you give the word, they'll swoop in."

"I don't plan to let anyone live that I come across. I've no time to play games."

"Understood, and I agree, but my agents will be able to keep the local law at bay while you save Miss Blake and your brother."

Tanner let loose a soft moan.

"I don't think I'll get to my brother in time. Murphy forced me to make a choice. I choose to save Sara."

"I can still send in those agents, Tanner."

"No, Lawson, they would only kill my brother quicker.

Besides, I know who he is now. I've met him, and if I'm right, he won't be easy to kill."

"Explain that."

Tanner did so, and heard Lawson reply with astonishment.

"Could he really be your brother?"

"I'm almost certain he is. It's why I was drawn to him the first time we met."

"Good luck, Tanner."

"Thanks, and Lawson, tell White I'll be available once this is over. I only wish I could help him now."

"He'll understand, and I'm giving him every assistance I can."

"It sounds like we both owe you a favor, and I always pay my debts."

"We help each other, Tanner. That's what friends do."

"Yes, and thanks again."

TANNER DROVE up to the ranch house while blowing his car's horn. As Doc appeared in the doorway of the barn, Tanner left his vehicle and ran up to him.

"I need your help, Doc."

"What is it?"

Tanner explained the situation quickly as he headed toward the stables.

"Why not call the cops?"

"That won't help. They'll have lookouts in place."

"Then they'll spot your car coming too."

"That's what I'm hoping for, and it's why I need your help."

Tanner explained his plan to Doc and saw the old man considering his request.

"Sure, I'll help. But we have to get you the right horse. How experienced a rider are you?"

"My father had me in the saddle with him as a baby and I've ridden ever since. I can handle a horse."

Doc pointed at a white horse.

"That's Blizzard. Maria finally broke him right before she went on her trip. Still, he's got plenty of spirit left in him, and man is he fast."

Tanner looked at his watch.

"Let's saddle him up. I'm running out of time."

~

SARA WOKE inside the old mill and wondered how she'd gotten there. The last thing she remembered was being inside her hotel room. Her wrists were cuffed behind her and she was seated on the floor with her back against a rusted, round metal support pole. She wore no gag, which told her that no one cared if she cried out for help.

In front of her and to her left, four men with rifles stood peering out a large window that was devoid of glass. There were no black suits or beards, so she guessed that they weren't with Ordnance Inc.

Trash coated the floor. When she attempted to stand, Sara felt pain, as grit and gravel poked the soles of her feet through the thin socks she was wearing.

One of the men heard her moving about. He was tall and gangly with large hands and a beak for a nose. He turned his head and smiled at her.

"Sleeping Beauty is awake, and just in time."

"In time for what?" Sara asked. Her voice sounded thick to her.

"We're going to kill your boyfriend. You're the bait," one

of the other men said. He had red hair that was going thin on top.

Sara spoke to the men, who were all staring at her.

"If any of you want to live, you'll release me and get away from here as fast as you can."

They laughed at her, with the redhead being the loudest. When he had finished his guffawing, he walked up to Sara.

"There are five of us. The four you see here and a guy with a scoped rifle. Your boyfriend doesn't stand a chance of even making it here. The second he turns off the highway and heads down the Old Mill Road he's a dead man."

"You keep calling him my boyfriend. Do you even know who it is you're here to kill?"

"All we know is that some guy messed with our boss, Moss Murphy. Once we kill the bastard, Murphy will send us on a free trip to Vegas."

"He's not just 'some guy'. You'll be going up against Tanner."

The men looked at each other with fear in their eyes, but then the redhead sent Sara a dismissive wave.

"Tanner lives in New York City. He wouldn't be hanging out in rural Texas."

The tall man cleared his throat.

"It doesn't matter. Tanner or not, my brother Mikey will kill him."

A radio squawked. The tall man took the unit off his belt and spoke into it.

"Is he here, Mikey?"

A tinny voice answered through the small speaker.

"His rental car is stopped out there on the highway, Glen. I can read the license plate but I can't see a face. He's got a hood pulled up."

"Any sign of cops?"

"None."

"Good, and hey, can you hit him from where you are?"

"I could try, but I doubt it. I mean I'm good with a rifle, but the highway is nearly a mile away. I'd rather wait until he makes his move and heads down the road."

"I hear you. Call us when he moves."

～

OUT ON THE HIGHWAY, Doc sat in Tanner's rental and wondered how he'd let Tanner talk him into helping him.

A sniper. Doc thought. *Tanner said there might be a damn sniper somewhere around the mill, and here I am sitting in the cross hairs.*

Doc checked the time on the dashboard again. Tanner had asked him to stay there for ten minutes. Doc didn't plan to stay there a second longer.

Only three more minutes, Doc thought, as sweat trickled down his back.

～

MILES AWAY, at the rear of the mill, Tanner approached a stream while riding Blizzard at full gallop. The horse was fast, the fastest one Tanner had ever ridden, he just hoped the beast had a heart to match his speed.

The mill had closed down back when Tanner's father was a boy. The Old Mill Road was the only way in by vehicle. Tanner had explored the dilapidated building several times while still a boy. He knew the terrain and was aware that the stream behind the mill property narrowed to only four feet wide at a certain point.

An old tree trunk once acted as a bridge across the stream, but Tanner assumed that had fallen into the water long ago. Still, a four-foot gap wasn't very wide.

What he had failed to consider was that the passage of time had eroded the banks of the stream. While the point he approached was still the narrowest section of the stream, it had grown to be over ten feet wide.

Tanner urged Blizzard toward the gap. The horse was a runner, not a jumper, but the beast caught sight of the water and seemed to run faster, apparently undeterred by Tanner's intent. As the horse leapt, Tanner was certain they wouldn't make it to the other side.

He was wrong. Blizzard cleared the gap with a foot to spare.

Tanner continued on toward the mill, but at a slower pace. After dismounting from the saddle, Tanner checked his watch. If Doc was doing his part, any snipers would be focused on his location at the front of the mill, while waiting for Doc to drive into their trap.

~

DOC SAW the time change on the clock and placed the car in drive. He then hesitated, as he figured a few more moments could only help Tanner. Besides, no one had taken a shot at him. After another minute passed, Doc drove off. He was feeling proud of himself for having gone the extra mile.

Good luck, Tanner.

~

THE TALL MAN'S radio squawked again. He pushed a button and spoke into it.

"It's almost noon. Is the guy coming down the road?"

"No, man, he just left. I guess he figured her fine ass wasn't worth getting killed over."

The tall man chuckled.

"I guess." He turned to look at Sara. "Tough luck for you."

One of the other men held up a hand.

"I hear something."

"Yeah," the redhead said. "Someone's walking around out there, maybe more than one."

The men raised their rifles and pointed them at the hole that had once been a large window. When they spotted what they'd been hearing, the tall man laughed.

"It's a damn horse. He probably wandered away from one of the farms around here."

"What if someone rode him here?" The redhead asked. He, along with the other men, were lowering their rifles.

"He'd have a saddle if someone was riding him," the tall man said.

Tanner popped up outside the window while holding a shotgun.

"I took the saddle off."

Tanner fired three shells at the men while aiming at their faces. He couldn't know if they were wearing vests and had no interest in getting in a firefight. The tall man was hit in the jaw, but fared better than his companions. He managed to hold on to his rifle, but before he could fire, Tanner blasted him in the face again.

All four men were down. Three moaned in agony, while the redhead was face down and pumping blood into the air from a nasty neck wound.

Tanner dived through the open window. A moment later, the wooden window sill splintered from a round fired by the fifth man, the sniper. After landing and transitioning into a shoulder roll, Tanner stood and sprinted over to Sara.

As usual, Tanner kept a concealed handcuff key on his person. He used it to free Sara, then felt her arms wrap around him.

Tanner caressed her in return, once again marveling at

how strong his love for her was. In fact, it proved strong enough to sacrifice a brother.

"Are you injured?" he asked.

"Other than sore wrists and feet, no."

"I still have to deal with the man who fired at me. Do you know if he's alone?"

"He is, but what about you? Who was driving our rental car?"

Tanner grinned.

"That was Doc acting as a decoy."

The radio squawked. Tanner plucked it off the tall man's belt and saw that all four men appeared to be dead, or damn near so. He pressed a button and spoke.

"If you want to live, leave now."

"Who is this?"

"The man you were supposed to kill."

"I'll kill you, asshole, but... let me talk to my brother."

"He's dead. They're all dead or dying."

A string of curses began but ended when the sniper's finger slipped off the button he was holding down. Tanner guided Sara over to a crumbling brick wall and told her to lay flat behind it.

A barrage of shots tore into the old mill, only one of them ricocheted off the bricks they took shelter behind.

When the shooting stopped, Tanner grabbed up two of the dead men's rifles.

"He's reloading. I'll head out the back and circle around. If he comes near you, kill him."

"Count on it," Sara said.

~

THE SNIPER WAS NAMED Michael Francis Riley. He was a street thug from Boston. The closest he had come to spending time in the country was when he and his brother used to burgle homes in the Boston suburbs.

It had never occurred to him that someone could approach the mill on horseback. Besides, there was a damn stream back there.

The man would free the woman and attempt to leave the same way. With the old mill in front of him, Riley had no view of the building's rear. He had to leave his sniper's perch and hunt the couple down. The man had also said that his companions were dead or dying. Riley hoped his brother was among the dying. If he killed the man and woman quickly, he might have time to get his brother to a hospital.

The terrain around the old mill was filled with scrub grass, weeds, and even a few cacti. The land undulated, and it unnerved Riley that he couldn't always keep the mill in sight now that he'd come down from the tree he'd been sitting in. He cursed that tree. The rough bark had made his ass hurt wicked awful.

He tried to stop crying, but tears fell anyway. Glen wasn't dying. He was dead. His big brother, dead. It didn't seem possible.

A soft sound came from his right, then another sound from his left. There were short hills on either side of him which hid whatever was on the other side. Riley scurried behind a gnarled tree for cover.

He heard more sounds, again, they came from both the left and the right. He figured the man and the woman had split up and were closing in on him. He couldn't figure how the woman could walk in her stocking feet across such rocky terrain. A second later he realized she wasn't, and that the man was alone.

From the right came the noise of something rustling among the scrub grass, followed by the sound of a horse whinnying. If the horse was on the right making all that noise, then the man was on the left, skulking, and moving stealthily as he sought to circle behind Riley and get the drop on him.

Riley stepped from cover with his rifle raised. He aimed at his left, as he waited to see a figure come over the small hill.

He never got the chance to fire. From the right, Tanner placed three shots into Riley. The sound startled the horse and he ran back the way he'd come, growing visible only as he galloped over a hill toward the left.

Tanner walked over to stare down at Riley's corpse. As he did so, he let loose another passable whinnying sound.

"N-e-e-eeeeeh!"

17

OUT OF TIME

Sara walked out of the mill as Tanner returned to it. She had taken a pair of sneakers off one of the dead men. They were laced tight, but still looked like clown shoes on her small feet.

"I found car keys, Tanner, but I have no idea where they parked."

"I do. I came across a pickup truck as I was riding here. It's behind the mill, and we need to leave now."

"What's going on?" Sara asked.

Tanner explained the situation as they drove toward the Alcott Motel. When Tanner looked at the time, he saw it was 12:19. He wondered if his brother was dead.

"You chose me over your brother?"

"Yes."

"I don't know what to say."

"My brother, I've already met him, Sara."

"Who is he? Do I know him?"

"No, but I've mentioned him to you."

Tanner explained how he knew his brother, and Sara smiled.

"I remember thinking that you seemed fond of the man. I also recall that you said he could handle himself well."

"He can, but so can you."

"I was drugged with something. I never got the chance to fight back."

"They may do the same thing to him."

A phone vibrated in Tanner's pocket. It was the phone that Moss Murphy left him. Tanner answered it and heard Murphy's voice.

"Since I can't get in touch with my men at the mill, I'll assume they're dead."

"You'd be right," Tanner said.

"Big deal. They meant nothing to me, but you signed your brother's death warrant. I'm sending you a video. I hope you enjoy it."

The call ended.

Tanner pulled over on the shoulder and saw that the phone had received an email with an attachment.

The words, LIVE FEED FROM NOON were printed as the video's heading.

The attachment loaded and revealed itself to be video from a helmet cam. The man wearing the camera carried a rifle, as did the bald man at his side. Off in the distance was the figure of a man. He was running for his life across a field of brown grass. Three other men came into view as a pickup truck pulled up beside the first two men.

Tanner wondered where the scene was taking place. The Alcott Motel was on a highway. There were no vast fields of grass nearby, just strip malls and scrubland.

He realized that Murphy had likely set a trap at the motel, believing that he would have rushed there first. If Murphy had placed five men at the mill as a precaution, he must have a small army at the motel, or perhaps he had rigged his brother's room with explosives.

What he was watching now were the men Murphy had actually employed to keep an eye on his brother. Having failed to fall for the trap at the motel, Murphy was going to make certain Tanner suffered. He had given the order to kill Caleb. The video Tanner was watching showed the men hunting Caleb down.

The bald man took to a knee and fired two shots at the fleeing figure in the video. The shots missed and the man kept running.

"That is one fast sonofabitch," the rifleman said.

"He can't outrun a truck," said one of the others.

The man wearing the camera and his bald companion clambered into the rear of the pickup. The truck lurched forward and went in pursuit.

As the truck went over a hill, Tanner realized that they were at the Reyes Ranch. His brother must have been visiting the family graves when they came after him.

The ranch house came into view, just a shape in the distance, but his brother's speed was such that he would reach it before the men in the truck. Caleb's speed was remarkable.

"Damn he can run," said the man with the camera.

Tanner watched his brother sprint past the house and head for the barn. As his brother shut the doors behind him. The truck pulled up in front of the barn and men piled out of it. Three of them had rifles that Tanner took to be M16's, while the other two carried AR-15's. As the bald man rushed toward the rear of the barn, the other men checked their weapons.

The man with the helmet cam took it off and smiled into the camera.

"He's as good as dead now, boss. We got him trapped like a rat."

The video ended.

Tanner tossed the phone into a cup holder, then whipped the pickup into a wild U-turn. He scattered vehicles on the other side of the roadway as he jounced across a grass road divider and merged with the traffic. Within seconds, he was weaving past cars at over a hundred miles an hour. As he neared the ranch, the phone vibrated.

Sara picked it up.

"There's a photo."

She opened the attachment and let out a moan.

"Oh, no."

Tanner screeched to a halt after careening off the exit that led to the ranch. Having taken the phone from Sara, he grimaced.

The photo showed his brother lying on the barn floor covered with blood. Standing over him was a grinning man wearing a long coat.

For the caption, the man, or perhaps Moss Murphy, had written three words.

Got the fucker!

The time stamp on the photo was many minutes old. Murphy's men would have already cleared out. Tanner's brother was dead.

Tanner sat staring ahead with a gaze that saw nothing. In the seat beside him, Sara wept.

His phone vibrated, his real phone. Tanner took it from his pocket and saw that Finn Kelly was calling.

"Yeah?"

"Tanner?"

"Yeah, Kelly."

"You all right, lad? You sound odd."

"Did that tip pan out?"

"Michael and Kate Barlow were in that hotel room in Brownsville, but they gave me the slip. The bastards left everything behind, including their luggage. I found a hidden camera in a travel clock. They must have known I was waiting in the room for them."

"Are you going to keep looking for them?"

"Until Joe tells me otherwise."

"Good. I want them, Finn. I want them bad."

"I'll do my best."

"One more thing. Moss Murphy is in the area. If you come across him let me know."

"I'll do that. Take care now."

As Tanner was putting away his phone, a police car sped by. Seconds later, two others whizzed past.

Tanner was glad to see it. He had been fearing that Doc might have died along with his brother, but if the cops had been called to the ranch, it was likely Doc who'd done so.

Tanner let out a sigh and felt Sara take his hand.

"I'm so sorry, baby."

Tanner looked at her and saw that she was crying.

"I guess I wasn't meant to have a brother."

"At least you knew him."

"Yes," Tanner said, and recalled the circumstances. He had been with Mr. White in California and hunting for a mutual foe named Brick. Caleb Parker had been going by another name then. Tanner realized why he had chosen it as an alias.

Caleb Parker had been using the name Stark, a name likely inspired by Stark, Texas. Stark was a thief who only stole from other thieves. Tanner had enjoyed the irony.

His first contact with Stark came when Stark saved his life, along with the life of Mr. White. Stark had tackled both men to the ground while risking himself, to save them from the crosshairs of a sniper. They had been on the trail of Brick, who had gathered a gang around himself and graduated to bank robbery.

Brick and Tanner had once crossed paths while Brick was assisting Ariana O'Grady, as she tried to get revenge against

Tanner. Mr. White had also had a confrontation with Brick, and so Tanner and White had teamed up to take Brick down.

As for Stark, he was looking to rob Brick and his men of their stolen wealth. Tanner had later saved Stark's life, as Stark assisted in the takedown of Brick and his crew.

Thinking back on that time, Tanner remembered sharing a drink with Stark as they got to know each other.

～

MR. WHITE, Tanner, and Stark had been seated together at a round wooden table in a bar that was headed toward closing time.

Tanner and Stark were drinking beer from frosted mugs, while White had red wine. Only Stark ate, as he indulged in a plate of cheese fries.

Mr. White was staring at Stark with a suspicious gaze, but Tanner trusted the man. That was unusual for Tanner, and he knew it was because Stark reminded him so strongly of someone from his past. Stark had reminded Tanner of his father.

"Is Stark your real name?" Tanner asked.

"No, and your name isn't really Tanner either."

"How do you know that?"

"I heard about the Tanners from an old cop I know, the thing is, he thought it was a myth."

"Most cops think I'm a myth. It works in my favor."

"Are you really a hit man?"

"I prefer 'trained assassin.'"

"And you took down a Mexican cartel?"

"I killed its leader, and had help doing it."

"Maybe you're not so bad, then."

"What's your game, Stark?" Mr. White asked.

Stark popped a fry into his mouth. After swallowing it, he spoke to White.

"My 'game' is robbing crooks. I hunt down the ones that make a big score and take it from them. Your game is chasing down serial killers, right? You're Dr. Jessica White's husband."

Tanner smiled as he asked a question.

"Do you really rob crooks?"

Stark grinned.

"I like giving them a taste of what they're dishing out."

"That sounds like a dangerous profession," Tanner said.

"Sometimes it gets hairy," Stark agreed.

~

TANNER HAD TAKEN an immediate liking to the cocky Stark, a rare occurrence for him, but now he knew why. After an ambulance followed the police cars, Tanner turned the pickup truck around and headed toward town.

1 8

HARD TO KILL

THE REYES RANCH, 12:04 P.M.

Doc STOPPED Tanner's rental halfway down the Reyes'
winding driveway as he heard the sound of rifle fire. He had
just returned from helping Tanner at the old mill, but it
seemed some new trouble was in the air.

The boy hired to muck out the stalls wasn't due until four
p.m., while the housekeeper Maria hired to cook and clean
didn't work on the weekends.

The ranch should be deserted. A pang of guilt passed
through Doc. Maria had trusted him to keep an eye on things
and he had deserted his post. Despite having left the ranch
unattended for a good reason, Doc still felt responsible for
whatever was going on.

He also blamed himself for being unaware that the Parker
family graves had been disturbed until long after the fact.
Some caretaker he was.

As he eased the car down the driveway, the ranch house
came into view. Doc saw a man run past on a beeline for the

131

barn and marveled at the man's speed. His wonder increased as the roar of an engine filled the air and a pickup truck with several armed men sped after the runner.

Doc sat there for a moment. If he backed out of the driveway slowly he could remain unnoticed and go off to get help. But what about the man who ran past him? Doc couldn't be certain, but he thought he might be the same young man he had spoken to out at the graves the previous morning.

If what that boy said was true, then he was the last surviving member of the Parker family. He wouldn't be surviving for long though, not if the men in the pickup got their hands on him.

After taking out his phone, Doc realized he didn't have a signal, as cell reception was spotty near the ranch. He had a choice to make. He could drive off and search for a cell signal to call the cops, or he could somehow attempt to help Parker.

Maria left me in charge. I can't just run off and hide.

Doc eased the car down the driveway with his heart pounding in his ears.

~

INSIDE THE BARN, Tanner's brother, Stark, was fumbling at the wires of an old tractor. It was an ancient John Deere and huge. Despite its age, the machine showed signs of recent use. Someone had employed it to move hay around, and a bale still sat in its loader bucket. The bucket attachment was made of thick metal and looked as old as the tractor.

He managed to hotwire the tractor and bring the rumbling motor to life. Shots peppered the barn door as he climbed into the tractor's seat. With the loader bucket raised, Stark only became aware that the doors had been opened when light flooded the barn's interior.

Stark got the tractor lumbering forward then climbed off the back of it. His hope was that he could escape out the barn's rear door while the men from the pickup were dealing with the moving tractor. He assumed they'd sent a man around the back to block his path, but better to deal with one man than with many.

After moving behind stacked bales of hay a wooden door came into view. The old door hung crookedly, and he could see movement beyond it. Stark rushed towards the door just as it opened.

A bald man wearing gray cargo pants and a Celtics sweatshirt stood in the open doorway. He had a rifle, but it was pointed downward. Stark sent three stiff fingers into the hood's throat, which caused the man to gag from a face turning red.

Stark took the rifle from the thug and used the weapon's barrel to give a hard jab into the man's side. A rib broke under the assault. The man moaned and slid along the doorjamb to sit on the floor. Behind Stark, the other men were shouting and firing at the rumbling tractor as they flattened the tires.

"He ain't here!" a voice cried out.

Stark rushed out the rear door and sprinted toward the front of the barn. He was hoping the men following him had left their truck unattended, if so, he could take it and flee the scene.

No such luck.

There was a man in the truck bed holding a rifle. When he spotted Stark, he grinned and swung the weapon toward him.

"He's out here!"

Stark was about to trade shots with the man when a blue streak appeared and rammed the back of the pickup truck. It wasn't a brutal impact, but it was enough to cause the man in the truck bed to lose his balance and fall out of it. The man landed on his head while issuing a loud groan, as his rifle skittered away.

"Get in, son!" Doc told Stark.

Stark sprinted to the passenger side and climbed in, as he did so, he noticed that the car was leaking fluid.

Doc put the car in reverse and sped back toward the driveway while looking over his shoulder, when he dared to glance forward, he saw that the remaining men were piling into the pickup truck to give pursuit.

After the car rounded a curve while scraping the fence on the right. Stark shouted for Doc to stop the vehicle.

Doc complied, but looked at him like he was mad.

Stark tumbled out the car with the rifle clutched in his hands.

"Go! Go!"

Doc moved in reverse again an instant before the pickup rounded the curve. The pickup driver's eyes grew wide at the sight of the vehicle blocking his path. The man slammed on the brakes and shifted into neutral; as he did so, Stark shot him.

The rifle round tore into the man's upper chest. His two remaining companions had been riding in the truck bed. Both men had been tossed atop the pickup's roof by the sudden stop. One man was perched up there well, but the other was fighting a losing battle. He slipped off the roof, slid down the windshield, and clutched onto a wiper blade. As the wiper tore loose from the stress of his weight, the man fell off the truck and landed at Stark's feet.

Stark kicked him on the side of the head with enough force to make the man flip over, while doing so, he kept his rifle aimed at the other man perched on the truck's roof. The man was aiming right back at him.

"Drop the rifle," Stark said.

"You drop your rifle. Our boss knows we're here. When he doesn't hear from us, he'll send more men."

Stark fired. His first round struck the man in the arm, which caused the return fire to go wide. His second shot shattered the man's left collarbone and made a nasty exit wound. The man slumped over and let out a scream of pain.

"Doc," Stark said. "I need you to help me again."

Still seated behind the wheel of the car, Doc was mesmerized by the scene playing out before him.

"Doc, grab one of these rifles and keep an eye on these three while I go back to the barn and check on the other two."

Doc broke from his trance and raised a hand to let Stark know that he'd heard him.

"By the way, Doc, thanks for saving my ass."

After getting out of the car, Doc picked up a fallen rifle and checked it over.

Seeing that Doc had things in hand, Stark moved back toward the barn. The man who had tumbled out of the truck was unconscious.

Stark took a knife from his pocket and cut off a sleeve from the man's shirt. He used it to bind the man's arms behind his back.

He heard the man he'd injured at the rear door before catching sight of him. The bald man was moaning and seemed to have trouble taking a breath.

As Stark approached him, the man spoke in a gasping voice.

"My rib broke... I think... I think it punctured a lung."

Stark left him where he was. He was going nowhere, as he could barely breathe.

As he came back out to the front of the barn, Stark saw that Doc had corralled the other three men and was marching them toward the barn at the point of a rifle. Two of the men were wounded, but the man he'd kicked on the side of the head looked fine. Stark spoke to him.

"Your friend there said your boss was waiting to hear from you. Who's your boss?"

"Moss Murphy."

Stark screwed up his face in a look of confusion.

"I never heard of Moss Murphy. Why the hell were you trying to kill me?"

"This wasn't about you. Murphy only wanted you dead to mess with Tanner."

"Tanner?" Stark said. "The Tanner who took down the Alvarado cartel?"

"Yeah."

Stark was more confused than ever, but he could figure it all out later. First, he had to keep Moss Murphy from sending more men after him. He turned to Doc. "That long coat you're wearing, take it off, will you? I have a plan."

A FEW MINUTES LATER, Stark lay on his back inside the barn. He was wearing the bloody shirt of one of the men he'd shot while holding a rifle pointed upward. The rifle was concealed behind the back of the man who stood over him, the man who was wearing Doc's long wool coat. If Stark pulled the trigger, the back of the man's head would take the round.

Doc used the thug's phone to snap a picture.

Afterward, Stark wandered about the area by the barn until he got a cell signal. Once he'd acquired a signal, he sent the photo to Moss Murphy, who forwarded it to Tanner. After binding up the other men, Doc went inside the house to use the land line to call the police.

Stark kept an eye on Murphy's men, who, other than their groans of pain, had become silent and sullen.

Doc returned from making the call and went about moving the vehicles from the driveway. The first police car arrived seconds later, as the sound of two more echoed in the distance. As the cops climbed out of their squad car, Stark asked Doc a question.

"Do you know Tanner?"

"Yeah, I just saw him earlier."

"I don't know what the hell is going on, but I think we should keep Tanner out of it."

Doc nodded his agreement, as the cops began to ask questions.

19

WELCOME HOME

An anonymous call to the police resulted in a dozen men being arrested at the Alcott Motel.

The men were armed and several had fully-automatic weapons. None of the men had gun permits or ID that stood up to scrutiny. The group was obviously up to no good, but to a man they refused to answer any questions and asked for a lawyer.

The men had been hired by Boston mob boss Moss Murphy at considerable expense. Murphy had been certain that Tanner would rush toward the motel to save his brother. He had underestimated Tanner's love for, and commitment to, Sara Blake.

Although Tanner still lived, Murphy had been filled with a sick satisfaction when he believed that his other men had killed Tanner's brother, Caleb. The sweetness of that victory turned bitter when Murphy heard from one of his men who had been arrested at the Reyes Ranch.

Caleb was still alive, Murphy had been deceived, and Tanner now had every reason in the world to want Murphy dead.

~

MICHAEL AND KATE BARLOW were headed toward Dallas in a car they had rented with their new identities.

As Finn surmised, they had accessed a hidden camera and saw that the Irishman was waiting for them in their hotel room.

Kate contacted Joy, the stripper at Johnny R's, and sent her a photo of Finn. Joy recognized Finn and told Kate that Finn Kelly worked for Joe Pullo. Joy also told Kate to lose her number.

Michael and Kate realized that somehow Pullo had become aware they had broken into his residence. If not for their habit of keeping a hidden camera in their hotel rooms, they might both be dead.

"That was too close," Kate said. She was driving, and frequently checking her mirrors for signs of a tail.

In the passenger seat, Michael was phoning Trevor Healy. If they had to go on the run, they could at least do so with their full fee paid. Healy didn't answer, so Michael left a message.

When Healy returned the call, he gave Michael the bad news.

"The client insists on waiting until the DNA results come back."

"Screw that. Didn't you tell me he decided to move forward without them?"

"He did so. The client failed to kill Tanner. I also learned that Tanner's brother survived as well."

"That means Tanner will be out to get him. If the client is dead, he can't pay up."

"I know. That's why I'm readying a Hammer Team to go after Tanner."

"Didn't you say the client hired a group of mercenaries to kill Tanner?"

"Yes, but they were rounded up by the police after an anonymous call tipped them off."

"You made that call, didn't you, Trevor?"

"Yes. Now the client will need to pay for one of our Hammer Teams."

"I hope the Hammer Team kills Tanner, but listen, we have another problem. Joe Pullo knows we broke into his place. One of his men was waiting for us in our room."

Michael heard Trevor sigh wearily.

"Can you help us with that, Trevor?"

"Not now. I've got even more problems with this other operation I'm running in Mexico."

"Damn. I wish we had located Tanner's mother, Marian Gant. Maybe we could use her somehow as a trade for our safety."

"Gant? Was that the woman's name?"

"Her maiden name, yeah. Why?"

Trevor sighed again.

"It complicates matters in this other operation I'm running."

"Can you help us, Trevor?"

"With Joe Pullo? No. If you somehow slipped up and were identified, that's on you two. We all take risks."

"We took risks to please your client."

"I know. Listen, call me in a few days. Maybe things will be resolved by then. I have to go."

The line went dead and Michael looked at his phone in disgust.

"We're on our own," he told his wife.

Once in Dallas, Michael and Kate Barlow, who were using the names of Roy and Rachel Thomas, bought new luggage, toiletries, and summer weight clothing.

Within hours, they would be on their way toward Rio De Janeiro.

~

TANNER ARRIVED at the ranch and found that no one was there but a kid mucking out the stalls. Tanner remembered him from his last visit to the ranch. The kid, Tommy, recalled him as well.

"Doc had to go into town and make a statement to the cops. He said he'd be back soon."

Tanner acknowledged Tommy with a nod, while examining the damage done to the barn doors.

"There was some kind of trouble out here today," the kid said. "I don't know what happened, but it sounds like somebody got hurt bad."

"Yeah," Tanner said.

Tanner was alone. He had left Sara at the hotel with a promise to fill her in later on what he learned. His brother had been killed, but perhaps his mother was still alive somewhere.

As he wandered over to the ranch house, Tanner saw the dent Doc had added to the front end of his car, and puzzled over how it had occurred.

Twenty minutes later, Tanner waved goodbye to Tommy, then watched as the kid rode off on his dirt bike.

Tanner wandered around to the stalls and was pleased to see that Blizzard had made his way back home. The animal was drinking from a trough and looked no worse for wear. Tanner secured him in a stall, then fed him one of the apples that was sitting in a basket.

"You're a hell of a horse."

Blizzard neighed and nodded as if he understood. After

leaving the stable, Tanner felt himself drawn toward the graves.

~

Doc and Stark were driving back from the police station. Neither of them had mentioned Tanner to the cops. Moss Murphy's men had said nothing other than to indicate that they understood their rights. They were professional criminals who let lawyers do their talking for them.

Stark let it be known that he wouldn't press charges if the damage done on the ranch was paid for in full. The police questioned him about why he was on the property in the first place, and Stark claimed he was chased there by Murphy's men.

Stark's ID was in his adoptive name of Caleb Knox. When it became known that he was the adopted son of the legendary Los Angeles police officer John Knox, the cops treated him like a minor celebrity.

Doc assured the officers that he would inform Maria Reyes about what happened and have her call them. When all the cops' questions had finally been answered, Doc and Stark were free to go.

"How do you know Tanner, Doc?"

Doc explained how he met Tanner while riding the rails, and how they had both come to work for the Reyes family.

"Tanner moved on, but I've been here ever since. I guess I'll still have a job until Maria sells the place."

"The ranch is for sale?"

"No, but I can see the signs. Maria's seldom here and her children are off building their own lives. I think it's just a matter of time before she tires of owning it."

"How often has Tanner come back here?"

"This is the first time. How do you know him?"

"We met out in California a few months ago."

Doc was driving an old Buick that Maria kept around to run errands in. The vehicle burned through oil at a furious pace, but it ran well otherwise.

Stark climbed out of the passenger seat and noticed the pickup truck Tanner had arrived in. Doc noted it as well, and recognized the saddle in the truck bed.

"That must belong to Tanner. This is the horse tack I loaned him earlier."

"I'll walk around and see if I can find him," Stark said.

"Bring him inside when you do. Right now, I'd better call Maria and let her know what's going on."

Stark watched Doc disappear into the ranch house before heading toward the barn. He stopped walking after a few feet and strolled off in a different direction, as something told him Tanner could be found at the graves.

~

TANNER KNELT before his mother's empty grave and wondered what had become of her. He then recalled the day that she had been laid to rest.

His grandfather had still been alive then. Young Cody had gripped Walter Parker's hand as his mother's casket was lowered into the ground. Standing beside him, Cody's father held his twin sisters in his arms, as he cried along with them.

Cody had used his free hand to wipe away tears, as he asked his grandfather why his mother had to die.

"We all die, Cody. What matters is how we lived. Your mother brought three great children into this world and made my son happy. She lived well, boy. We'll always remember and cherish her."

~

TANNER'S HAND was moving toward his concealed holster before he realized he was doing it, then he became aware that someone was approaching.

It was a man, but Tanner couldn't see him well, as mottled sunlight obscured the man's details while he ambled under the leaves of a tree.

Tanner had been swallowed up in memory, but decades of training and living on the edge kept him from ever becoming totally unaware of his surroundings.

He cleared his throat and stood. As the man grew closer, Tanner realized he was looking at Stark. The sense of joy that passed through him from finding his brother alive was palpable. He greeted Stark with a huge grin.

"You survived Murphy's goons."

"With help from Doc," Stark said.

Stark stopped walking when he was still several feet from Tanner.

"You have my mother's eyes, Tanner. When we met in California I thought that was just a coincidence... now I'm not so sure."

Tanner closed the gap between them, as he did so, he came even with his own empty grave. He pointed at it.

"The body taken from that grave was not Cody Parker."

Stark cocked his head.

"How do you know that?"

"Because I'm Cody Parker. I'm your brother, Caleb."

Stark's breathing increased.

"My family is dead."

"I survived. The boy in that grave was named Pablo. He was a Mexican orphan. Our father took him in and gave him a home after our sisters found Pablo hiding in the barn."

Stark stared at him.

"Alonso Alvarado, was he the one who came here and

killed everybody? All I ever found out was that it was a cartel member named Martillo."

"Martillo was Alonso Alvarado's nickname. When he was a young man, he liked to kill with a Martillo, a hammer."

"Is that why you went to Mexico to kill him... to avenge our family?"

"Yes."

Stark's eyes had grown moist.

"Are you really Cody Parker?"

Tanner opened his arms.

"I'm your brother, Caleb. I'm Cody."

Stark went to Tanner. After a brief embrace, the two men separated and stared at each other.

Tanner gazed back toward their mother's empty grave.

"What happened to Mom, Caleb?"

Stark's face reddened in anger.

"It's not what, but who, and the who was her own sick, twisted brother, a man named Billy Gant."

"I recently learned that Gant faked her death."

"Yes."

"Caleb, is our mother alive?"

Stark wiped away tears.

"I'm sorry, no, she died while I was still a boy."

A small sound of grief escaped Tanner, making him realize that he'd been hoping for a second miracle.

"Caleb?"

"Yes, Cody?"

Tanner gestured around at the ranch.

"Welcome home, Brother."

20

THE TRUTH COMES OUT

"Our mother brought me to Stark when I was eight. Having been kept a prisoner inside her brother's compound for so long, she had heard nothing about what happened here."

Stark was filling Tanner in on his past while they walked back to the ranch house.

"To say she was devastated by discovering the burnt remains of her home would be an understatement. Still, she had hope that everyone had gotten out all right. That was when we visited an old friend of Mom's, Emily something. Anyway, Cody, that was when we learned the truth."

Stark's sad features brightened.

"She really loved you, you know? All I heard growing up was Cody this and Cody that. She made you sound bigger than life, and I'll be damned if you aren't."

Tanner smiled back at him.

"She claimed I had a rambunctious spirit, but our father said I was hardheaded and couldn't wait to grow up. They were both right."

Stark stopped walking.

"What was our father like? I know mother loved him."

"He was a simple man who only wanted the best for his family. To die the way he did, forced to watch his children be murdered… and to be unable to help them… it was a tragedy."

"Mom said I look like him."

"You favor him, and you have his green eyes."

They returned to the ranch and found Doc sitting on the porch waiting for them. Tanner thanked Doc for all the help he had given him, and came to a decision.

"Doc, I have a story to tell you."

~

"CODY PARKER?"

"Yes." Tanner said.

Doc squinted at him.

"Frank Parker's boy?"

"That's the one."

"Damn, son. I brought you into this world, you and your sisters."

"Yes, sir."

Doc stared at Caleb, and a smile crossed his face.

"I saw Frank's influence in this boy, and if memory serves, you have your mother's eyes, Tanner. Well, I'll be damned. The Parker family is making a comeback."

"We needed to stay dead as long as Alonso Alvarado was alive. He's dead now," Tanner said.

Doc looked around.

"By all rights, this is your land."

"Maybe, but I won't be taking anyone to court to get it back. Caleb told me that you think Maria might be willing to sell it?"

"Yeah, the ranch barely broke even last year. Maria

wanted to raise her children here. She's done that. She also knows that neither Romina or Javier want to be ranchers. Besides, she's marrying a man who already owns a home here in town."

"Thanks for the info," Tanner said.

The sound of a car engine came from the driveway and a taxicab appeared. The woman who emerged from it paid her fare and walked up onto the porch. It was Sara. Tanner had called and told her of Stark's survival. She had been thrilled to hear the news.

Tanner greeted her with a kiss and introduced her to Stark.

"Sara Blake, this is my brother, Caleb."

"I'm very glad to meet you," Sara said, to a smiling Stark. "And I see a resemblance when you smile. Tanner has a great smile, although he seldom displays it."

"It's on display tonight," Tanner said. It was true. In fact, he had seldom been happier.

∾

Moss Murphy stepped out onto the balcony of his Dallas hotel room and called Trevor Healy.

He was furious that his men had not only failed to kill Tanner, but disgusted by the debacle caused when they went after Tanner's brother. Lawyers had to be called in to keep the cops away from his door, and he still might end up being interrogated.

His position as the head of the Boston mob was tenuous after the devastation Tanner had inflicted, in which Murphy had lost a number of his best street soldiers, along with his house.

Finn Kelly had also defected to join Joe Pullo in New York. It wasn't until Kelly was gone that Moss appreciated how much Finn had done for him. Kelly had been vital in keeping things running smoothly.

Add to that the exorbitant sum that Joe Pullo had insisted on to avoid going to war, and Murphy was on one hell of a losing streak.

But it was Tanner's ruthless attack on Moss' son, Liam, which had sent him on his current path of vengeance.

From the start, Moss knew he had to hit Tanner where it would hurt the most. That meant he had to go after the man's family. An eye for an eye and a tooth for a tooth.

Discovering that the man had no family seemed too unlikely to Murphy, and he had paid a small fortune to Ordnance Inc. to unearth a brother. Tanner's brother proved himself to be a hard man to kill, and he damned near killed two of Murphy's men.

Tanner would be coming for Murphy. That was certain. So now it had come down to kill or be killed.

Moss Murphy heard Trevor Healy answer his phone. When he spoke, there seemed to be a touch of amusement in Healy's tone.

"Hello, Mr. Murphy, I see your plans for Tanner didn't go as you'd wished."

"No shit. How can you help me with that?"

"Ordnance Inc. has an option for when all else fails. We call them Hammer Teams. I just happen to have one standing by in case you wish to employ them."

"How many men to a team?"

"Seven men and one woman. The woman is just as deadly as the men, but she can also be useful as a spy or a diversion. All the women on the Hammer Teams are beautiful."

"What will it cost me?"

Trevor mentioned a figure, then added a caveat.

"That price is to be paid immediately, along with everything else you owe us."

"Yeah, yeah, but do you guarantee they'll kill Tanner?"

"No, but they'll be highly motivated. It's understood that Tanner doesn't take prisoners."

"Have this team ever failed?"

"Not once in sixteen assignments. Their combination of guile, misdirection, and brute force is hard to beat."

There was a pause in the conversation as Murphy thought over his options. If the Hammer Team lost their battle with Tanner he would need to go into hiding. There would be no way that Tanner wouldn't get to him if he returned to Boston.

Murphy closed his eyes in pain. His son had begun this nightmare. Liam had tried to fly too high too fast and got his wings clipped. He loved Liam, but his son's ego was soon to cost him everything... unless Tanner died.

"I'll authorize the payment. Make sure they kill Tanner."

"You made the right choice," Healy said.

"There is no other choice," Murphy said.

In truth, there was another choice, although Murphy would hate to admit it.

Deep down, he thought he could save himself both time and money by placing his gun in his mouth and pulling the trigger. No doubt it would be a kinder death than the one Tanner would dish out to him if the Hammer Team failed.

21

TIME'S ARROW

S<small>ARA'S LONG HAIR SWIRLED ABOUT HER AND</small> T<small>ANNER AS THEY</small> kissed goodbye.

The wind produced by the helicopter blades also caused dust to swirl, lending the setting sun an ominous color. Tanner had called Thomas Lawson and asked that he ferry Sara, Stark, and Doc to a safe location. He would stay behind on the ranch alone and wait for Moss Murphy to make his next move.

"Let me stay with you," Sara said.

"No. I want you and Caleb somewhere safe."

"You know Murphy will send more men to kill you."

"I do, and you know what happens to people who try to kill me."

"I'll still worry. Mr. Lawson said that Ordnance Inc. had the resources to send a team of killers after you."

"That's what I'm hoping. If I take out their best, Ordnance Inc. will think twice before helping people like Murphy come after me."

"What if they seek revenge for themselves?"

"Lawson said it wasn't their style. They're strictly hired help."

Sara kissed him.

"Please be careful."

"I'll call you when it's over."

Sara joined Stark and Doc on the helicopter. Stark hated leaving Tanner alone as much as Sara did. Although he was brave and not afraid of facing violence, Stark was no killer. Robbing thieves as a sort of modern day Robin Hood hadn't prepared him to face a squad of trained killers.

He was aware that he had been damn lucky to survive his encounter with Murphy's men. Murphy wouldn't be fool enough to think sending thugs against Tanner would ensure the hit man's death.

He would send the best he could find, and given his recent track record of using them, Murphy would once again turn to Ordnance Inc.

The helicopter lifted into the air and Tanner felt better knowing that he wouldn't have to worry about those he cared about.

Thomas Lawson had also sent Tanner a crate of supplies, along with a small measure of backup.

An all-terrain vehicle approached Tanner from across a field. He walked over to speak to the Homeland Security agents in it. To them, he was Thomas Myers, and they were sent there to enhance the ranch's security.

The black-clad agent behind the wheel of the vehicle smiled at Tanner while handing him a package that contained a laptop, tablet, and a cell phone. His name was Agent Dowell.

"Mr. Myers, the concealed cameras, motion detectors, and the lights are being installed. The work should be completed by 2200 hours. Mr. Lawson assured us that you were familiar with the setup and that you needed no instruction in operating the equipment. Is that correct, sir?"

"It is."

"Excellent," Agent Dowell said, as his eyes took in the items Tanner had been going over. When he spotted the Barrett sniper rifle, the man's eyebrows rose up a fraction. "I see you're expecting guests."

"It's likely," Tanner said.

The agent looked Tanner over, then threw a thumb at his silent companion.

"Agent Erickson and I could stick around until morning if you'd like. Mr. Lawson said to give you whatever help you needed."

"Thanks for the offer, but my guests may not visit if they think I'm not alone."

"Understood, and good luck."

The agents drove off to continue their work while Tanner went back to checking his inventory. When he first met Thomas Lawson, Tanner had thought him a cut above the usual government bureaucrat, but Lawson was something else altogether.

Thomas Lawson's clout within the government was unequalled. Lawson claimed it was because he got things done. The fact that Lawson had enlisted Tanner, an assassin, on more than one occasion wasn't unusual. The government often paid people to kill, and bred their own professional killers as well.

What was remarkable, was that Lawson acted alone, and seemingly under his own authority. In Tanner's experience, anything remotely governmental had layers upon layers of bureaucracy and self-important people with titles after their names. If Thomas Lawson had a title, Tanner had never heard it used.

Lawson had power.

He was using that power on Tanner's behalf and Tanner was grateful for it.

As a younger man, Tanner never thought he needed anyone other than his mentor, Spenser. Now, in his late-thirties, with decades of experience and hard-won wisdom, he knew that wasn't true.

After losing his family, Tanner had decided to be alone forever rather than risk the pain of loss again. And yet, there were women who entered his heart over the years and built a home there. Love, like death, was inevitable. You could fight it, run from it and deny it, but in the end, you could not avoid it, not if you had a soul.

Time also had a way of working on you, of wearing you down and making you crave what you always denied yourself. Alexa had stripped away the last of Tanner's resistance to love, but she had not been willing to accept him, not all of him.

Sara Blake both loved him and accepted him. That acceptance was in itself a form of love.

Yes, time changed everyone, as well as everything.

He had spoken with Spenser on the subject a short time ago in Wyoming. It had been past midnight, and they had sat beside the fireplace drinking whisky, while discussing the Tanners who came before them.

~

"IT CAN'T CONTINUE," Spenser had said. "Not the way it's always been."

"What can't continue?"

"Us, Cody, being a Tanner. If there is a Tanner Eight, he'll have a whole new world to deal with. Facial recognition is soon to be as common as surveillance cameras in convenience stores. There's software being developed that will be able to identify someone even if they're wearing a mask. Add to that the backscatter technology that can x-ray an entire vehicle. Such machines are being installed at tunnel entrances and inside office buildings. Try getting a weapon past something like that. In that sort of world, you can't gun and run, not when your movements will be tracked every step of the way by an infrared drone."

"If all that happens, it won't be anytime soon."

"Maybe, Cody, or it may be sooner than we think."

Tanner hadn't given Spenser's words much thought, but what Spenser had said was true. Technology was changing the world. It was making whole segments of it obsolete, be they legal or illegal.

Brick & mortar retail stores were fading and the smart retail management had a strong online footprint. Criminals that at one time would have robbed a payroll truck were now partnering with computer hackers to break into bank accounts. A new world was emerging. If the tradition of Tanner was to continue, changes would have to be made.

~

TANNER PLACED his mind back on the business at hand and continued to inventory his supplies. There was a fake arm cast that would slip on and off easily. It had a small gun concealed within it.

Lawson warned Tanner that Ordnance Inc. was known to use guile as well as brute force. The phony cast might come in handy if Tanner needed to employ his own deceptions.

He removed a package of a hundred plastic zip ties in various sizes from the crate. They had many uses and could double as handcuffs. Beneath the zip ties were several boxes of spare ammo and extra magazines.

At the bottom of the crate Tanner found a small package.

It held a GPS tracker on a chain that looked like a pendant. The pendant had a button on top. There was also a note.

PRESS THE BUTTON AND HELP WILL ARRIVE – T.L.

T.L. was Thomas Lawson.

Tanner smiled. It was good to have friends in high places.

2 2

HAMMER TIME

LAWSON'S PEOPLE LEFT THE RANCH AT 9:56 P.M.

At 12:17 a.m. a car stopped out on the road. Steam poured out from beneath its hood. A young woman emerged from the driver's seat. She was blonde and wore a waitress uniform. After raising the hood, she let out a string of curses as the steam stung her hand.

The microphones and cameras Lawson's people installed were top quality. Tanner could hear every word she uttered as he watched her on a laptop.

After taking out her cell phone, the woman tried unsuccessfully to make a call. Cell service out at the ranch was sporadic, and she was unable to connect. She sighed, hugged herself, shivered slightly, and looked around. When she spotted the entrance to the ranch she started toward it.

TANNER OPENED the door before she could ring the bell.

He put her age at about twenty-five. The eyes were blue, the face beautiful, and her figure filled out the waitress uniform curvaceously. She had buttoned her gray uniform up to its white collar against the chill of the night, and its fabric bore the stains of the day's work.

A name tag sat above her left breast. The tag was white with a gold border. The words, JIMMY'S DINER was printed in small letters across the top border while the name ASHLEY was in a large script in the center. The name tag looked worn and there were small scratches across its surface.

She smelled of grease, looked tired, and wore sneakers with thick, slip-resistant soles. Everything about her, from her inexpensive watch to the smudge of ketchup on her collar, said that she was a waitress who had just finished a shift at work.

She looked up at Tanner, offered an apologetic smile, then spoke with a regional accent.

"I'm so sorry to bother you, especially at this hour, but my damn car broke down out there on the road."

"No problem, I was still up."

"My phone can't get a signal. Can I use your house phone to call my boyfriend?"

"Yeah, is he waiting up for you?"

The woman laughed.

"Curtis? No, he's asleep by now, but I'll be damned if I'll waste money on a cab."

Tanner pointed out the phone and the woman went to it and dialed a number. Her end of the call sounded genuine. As she talked, Tanner used a computer tablet to check the security cameras. He saw no signs of movement on any of them, nor did any of the motion sensors light up.

When the woman ended the call, she released a sigh.

"Thanks, Curtis should be outside in about ten minutes. Our apartment is just over by the new park."

The park was new. It was a fact that an area resident

would know and acknowledge in conversation. A stranger would have simply said that they lived near *the* park. If this woman was with Ordnance Inc., she was damn good.

Tanner was damn good too. While she'd been walking along the ranch's long and winding driveway, Tanner had done a bit of stage dressing. He had put on the phony cast and placed a bottle of pills out in the open where they could easily be seen.

The pills were from Maria Reyes' medicine cabinet. They were what remained of the painkillers Maria had been prescribed when she'd had a root canal. Tanner had also mussed his hair on one side, as if he'd been sitting with his head resting on his arm. The overall impression was that of a man not at his peak.

Tanner smiled pleasantly at the woman in acknowledgement of her comments, but said nothing. The woman pointed at her name tag.

"I'm Ashley."

"Nice to meet you, Ashley. I'm Tom."

"You got a great place, Tom. You live here alone?"

"No, in fact, I'm just visiting. The ranch belongs to friends."

"Oh."

They were silent. Tanner looked relaxed and acted like he was stifling a yawn. Ashley gazed about nervously, as most young women would when alone in a secluded house with a man they didn't know. When she looked at Tanner again, she had a question on her mind.

"I hate to be more of a bother, but can I use your bathroom?"

"Sure, there's one down the hall there on the left."

"Thank you. I swear, after that, I'll leave you in peace."

Ashley moved toward the bathroom, entered it, and locked the door. She spent an appropriate amount of time in there. After the gurgle of the toilet flushing, there followed the sounds of someone washing their hands.

Tanner again checked for signs of intruders and found none. He went online and located a webpage for Jimmy's Diner. It was a single page boasting they had the Best Burgers in the County. There were photos of food, but none of people. Tanner did find information at the very bottom of the page.

Proprietor: James Denning – Cooks: Oscar, Mike, and Benny – Wait Staff: Jenny, Barbara, Beth, Michaela, Annie, Ashley, and Camila.

So, there was an Ashley working at Jimmy's Diner. The question still remained to be answered if she was the same woman in the bathroom.

When she returned, Ashley headed to the door to leave. She sent Tanner a wide smile.

"Thank you so much, Tom. Come by Jimmy's Diner and I'll see you get a free meal."

"I may do that," Tanner said.

Ashley left the house to wait in her car for her boyfriend.

It was a short wait. The boyfriend was a young guy who looked to be in shape. He wore a colorful sweatshirt that had the word STAFF on the front and the name of a popular fitness center on the back.

Ashley gave her boyfriend a kiss before walking with him to stare down inside the engine compartment of her car.

The boyfriend went to the rear of his red pickup truck, where he grabbed two gallon-size jugs of water. After he emptied them into the car's coolant system, he told Ashley to start her car.

Ashley let out a little cheer when the engine ran and no steam came out from under the hood.

"That's a temporary fix," the boyfriend said. "Let's get home before the water leaks out."

Ashley sent him an OK sign to signal her agreement. As the boyfriend drove off in his pickup truck, Ashley followed behind him. The road outside the ranch grew silent once more.

Lawson had informed Tanner that Ordnance Inc. offered their clients many services. One of those services was elite groups of mercenaries they called Hammer Teams. Lawson's intel hadn't carried the information that Hammer Teams employed women as operatives, but Tanner thought it likely.

Was the woman he'd met a waitress who just happened to have car trouble within sight of the ranch, or was she part of a Hammer Team sent in to assess the situation?

If the latter were true, she had learned that Tanner was alone, that it appeared he had been injured during an earlier confrontation, was impaired by painkillers, and fighting fatigue. If the former were true, then Ashley's appearance was just a coincidence.

Tanner's mentor had taught him many things while he'd been training him. Included in the training was wisdom and the occasional warning.

"Remember, Cody, taking things at face value can kill you."

Tanner remembered, and he wasn't a big believer in coincidence.

≈

THE WOMAN TANNER knew as Ashley followed her "boyfriend" only several hundred yards before they turned left and headed down a gravel road. The road was a track that led to a weather-beaten barn on the property that sat across the road from the Reyes Ranch.

No one had lived on the property for months. The former owners had gone bankrupt and the cattle ranch was in foreclosure. The Ordnance Inc. Hammer Team was using the location as an operation's base.

After wiping them down, the pair left their stolen vehicles parked beside two black Jeeps used by the Hammer Team. They had employed the car and pickup truck like props as they did reconnaissance on Tanner. Once the operation was completed, the stolen vehicles would be burned with the help of an accelerant.

The fire would eliminate any trace of DNA evidence left in the vehicles. It would also remove any damning DNA that might be found on the body inside the waitresses' trunk.

They walked in silence up a slight hill and toward the old barn. Nearby, a huge black man stood watch. He was wearing the newest generation night-vision monocular and cradling a rifle. He answered their waves with a nod and went back to scanning his surroundings. At the rear of the barn, another man was keeping watch.

Hammer Teams didn't use the NATO Alphabet designations as the lower-tier teams did. They used numbers when they were around others and working. Number One was the leader, while Numbers Two through Eight were equals. But they were a close-knit team and knew each other's names.

Ashley's real name was Scarlett.

The team leader looked her over. He was a former Marine, and at forty-one, the oldest of the group.

"Glad to see you're still in one piece, Scarlett. Our target has quite the reputation."

"So do we," Scarlett said with her native Australian accent. As she spoke, she unzipped her waitress uniform. After stepping out of it and kicking off the sneakers, she was clad only in a matching pair of red bra and panties, along with white socks. Her male team members looked her over, while trying not to be too obvious about it.

The view was available for a short time, because she was soon donning a black jumpsuit. Over the jumpsuit would go a tactical vest with multiple pouches.

When they engaged Tanner, Scarlett's job would be to haul along their spare ammo, medical supplies, and tactical gear. She would also act as a medic if needed, since she had the necessary training.

The leader, Mitch, spoke to her as she dressed.

"Let's hear your report."

"He's alone. The thermal scanner in my purse picked up only two human heat signatures, his and my own. I know the range on the handheld device is low, but I doubt anyone is hiding far out in the fields."

"What's Tanner's condition?"

Scarlett grinned.

"You're gonna love this. His left arm is in a cast and I think he's taking painkillers. If I had to guess, I'd say he's not expecting any trouble tonight. It wouldn't surprise me if he went to sleep."

The team leader greeted that news with a worried frown.

"What, Mitch? I thought you'd be happy."

"It's good news. It's just that this guy is supposed to be something truly special. He already single-handedly took out a five man team the client sent against him."

The young man who had pretended to be the waitress' boyfriend let out a laugh.

"Mitch, those guys were some cheap ass Boston street thugs. I'm not impressed by Tanner taking them out. Besides, it looks like they injured him too."

"Yeah, that's what it looks like, but Scarlett also looked like a poor waitress whose car broke down."

"Okay, I see your point, but either way, the dude's alone over there."

Mitch began walking around the inside of the barn. He

always thought better when he walked. Trevor Healy had given Mitch everything they had learned about Tanner. Mitch knew that much of it was speculation or based on second-hand accounts, but the bottom line told him one truth.

Tanner was not a man you wanted to take lightly, not if you wanted to go on living. After doing several circuits around the barn, Mitch stopped walking.

The team leader wore a satellite phone on his belt. It alerted him that he had a call from one of his men. It was from the man keeping watch out front.

"What's up, Brian?"

"There's a spot near the road where I can see the top right corner of the front windows."

"Of the house where Tanner is staying?"

"Yeah, and the lights just went out. I think the asshole has gone to bed."

"Nice catch, but stay frosty."

"Oh yeah, my guard is never down."

When the call ended, the team leader spoke to Scarlett.

"Brian said the lights went out over there."

"I told you Tanner looked tired. After all, Mitch, he's almost as old as you."

"Ha, ha," Mitch said. He looked at his people one by one and came to a decision.

"We'll hit Tanner at four a.m. and use everything we have. I want to leave that house in ruins with Tanner's corpse inside it. I don't want to give that fucker an inch."

The members of the Hammer Team cheered their leader's decision, they then went about checking their gear and weapons again.

While they were doing that, their team leader was running through everything in his mind, looking for a weakness in the way they were handling the operation. He saw none. Sending Scarlett in had been the only risk he'd taken. It had paid off well.

Mitch smiled as confidence strengthened his resolve.

They were eight well-trained experienced team members who complemented each other and had a string of spectacular successes behind them. They were armed with the latest weapons, had the will to use them, and had defeated superior odds on more than one occasion. One man, any one man, be he exceptional or not, should fall before their onslaught.

All of that was true, except for the first part.

They were no longer eight.

They were down to seven.

Tanner was in their midst.

23

NAILED!

After watching the waitress' car drive off, Tanner turned the volume up high on the motion sensor alarms.

Lamps throughout the house had been plugged into programmable timers. Tanner reset them so that they would go off in a sequence that made it appear he was shutting off lights in preparation to go to bed.

Confident that he would receive a warning if anyone approached the house, Tanner removed the fake cast and put on a concealable ballistic vest under a black long-sleeved shirt. His cargo pants were also black. He placed a spare magazine in each of his many pockets.

After strapping a blue-steeled machete in an ebony sheath across his back, Tanner was ready to go. His planned destination wasn't far. He just wanted to walk out to the street.

He also wanted to keep breathing. To accomplish both tasks he needed to be cautious.

Tanner entered the basement, disabled the alarm on the storm cellar doors, then stepped out into the night.

Thanks to a row of thick hedges, there was no view of the

storm doors from anywhere else but the side yard. Tanner stayed low and used the hedges for concealment. Afterward, he used a leather head mount to make his night-vision monocular hands-free.

Finding no signs of anyone nearby, Tanner ventured along the hedges until he was looking out on a field at the left side of the house. There were several forms moving out there, looking green in the monocular, but all were too small to be human.

Tanner sprinted on a diagonal line until he was behind the shelter of a tree, then repeated the process. Three minutes later, he was out on the road and searching the street with his natural eye.

He found what he'd been looking for. It was water. The waitress' leaking radiator had left a trail behind in the dry street.

Tanner had to conceal himself only once on the quiet road when two young couples went by in an old Buick with the stereo blasting. After they'd passed, he resumed his stalking and found that the fading water trail made an abrupt left turn onto the property of the ranch across the way.

Tanner smiled. The woman, whoever she was, was excellent. She'd had him believing she was a local waitress. However, taking things at face value was foolish, and verification had to be made.

She had not passed her verification. Whoever sent her to check him out had been a little too cute. Too clever by half is how Tanner's grandfather would have put it.

A busted automobile radiator was a good ploy, but they would have been better off had they feigned battery trouble. There would have been no trail to follow.

Tanner concealed himself in shadows and thought over the situation.

They had to assume he had bought the woman's act. They

may even believe his own act and think that he had an injured arm. They would also presume he was alone, which he was, but they would also have no reason to believe he knew their location.

They had superior numbers, but he would have the element of surprise. Between the two advantages, Tanner would take surprise every time.

The question then arose of how long would they wait to strike?

They wouldn't come right away, no, they would wait, and in the deep of the night they would come with full force and fury.

Tanner took inventory. He had three guns, including a small pistol in an ankle holster that held only five rounds. The other two guns were the same model Glock. He estimated he had over a hundred and fifty rounds between the loaded weapons and the spare magazines he carried. Add to that a machete and two knives and Tanner felt ready to rock.

He eased the machete from its sheath and moved with the stealth of a shadow.

∼

AFTER FINDING the Hammer Team's vehicles, including the stolen ones used by the waitress and her boyfriend, Tanner had come across the barn.

He knew the property well and thought of it as The Double-Eagle Ranch. As a boy, he had played and hunted rabbits on it with a kid named Boyd LaMar.

The property had changed hands since then. Like other things in Stark, it had fallen on tough times. Tanner was hunting on the property once again, but this time the stakes were higher.

~

A BLACK MAN with a night-vison monocle hanging around his neck was speaking to someone on a satellite phone. The man had spotted the timer turning off the lights at the Reyes Ranch. As Tanner hoped someone would, the man assumed it meant that he had laid down for the night.

Tanner had used the sound of the call to ease his way closer to the man, who was leaning back against the rusted remains of what had once been a farm truck. The tires were flat and the windshield cracked.

Once the call ended, the black man gazed across at the Reyes Ranch while using the night-vision monocle. After removing a canteen off his belt, the big man leaned his head back to swallow the cool liquid he was gulping.

Tanner rushed him at that moment. The guard detected the movement, but he had a mouthful of water and his gun hand held the canteen to his lips. Liquid shot out the man's nostrils as he choked on the water and released the canteen. As that was happening, Tanner's machete ripped open the guard's throat and damn near severed his head.

A gurgling sound preceded the noise of the blood splashing against the old truck. Tanner had rushed behind the man. His intent was to ease the body to the ground to reduce the noise its falling would make. A more important consideration was that the big man's body could act as a shield if one of his partners happened along.

The man fell quietly enough, but then thrashed about wildly. Tanner was surprised, he doubted the man had much blood left inside him. The noise ended as swiftly as it began.

Tanner heard nothing, but then voices were raised in what sounded like a cheer. Whatever they were celebrating inside the barn was a mystery to Tanner, but a clear indication they had no clue he was there.

He moved on to scout the rest of the perimeter and came across a second man at the barn's rear.

~

THE TREE, *the old shed, the stone bench, then back to the tree,* Tanner thought, as he watched the man at the rear of the barn patrol his area.

He was a thin young guy with a heavy shadow of black stubble and alert ever-shifting brown eyes. He wore black jeans along with a black hoodie, but kept the hood down.

Tanner was lying behind the base of a tree and watching the man walk the same short route over and over. The guard appeared restless, but could just as easily be the sort that never sat still.

The first stop on his route was an old oak tree with lovers' initials carved into it. Once the man reached that spot on the right, he made a sharp left and headed eighty feet to a wooden shed that termites had feasted on. It was a shed in name only; in reality, it was a pile of wood about to fall over. As he passed the shed, the sentry made another left which sent him back to his starting point, a stone bench.

The man never sat, he just kept moving, but once, he did pause to pop a mint in his mouth.

When Tanner thought he had the timing down, he rushed across the dry grass to the tree as the man was reaching the shed.

He couldn't help but make some sound while moving across the dry weeds, but it was minimal, since he used the path that had already been created by the guard. Crouched behind the tree with a gun in one hand and the machete in the other, Tanner waited for the man to come back toward the tree.

He didn't come.

Tanner waited a little longer, then slid the corner of his left eye past the edge of the tree.

The sentry was sitting on the stone bench and tying his boot. When he finished with that, he slid a Ka-Bar knife from its sheath and headed toward the tree.

Tanner was perplexed. If the man was aware he was behind the tree, then why not call out and alert the others? And a knife? The man had an AR-15 slung over his back.

The answer came a few moments later as the scratching sounds began. The guy was carving his and his girl's initials into the tree.

Tanner moved out from behind the tree and brought the machete down on the top of the man's head. The sharp blade split open his skull.

"That tree is only for locals," Tanner chided in a whisper. He needn't have made the admonishment. The man was already dead.

~

INSIDE THE BARN, the team leader, Mitch, was checking his cell phone after receiving a text message from Trevor Healy. It was bad news.

He answered Trevor's text with one of his own, then spoke to his troops.

"That other operation in Mexico went all to hell. Trevor Healy said he left early to see to our deployment here. If not for that, he might have died too."

Scarlett gaped at him.

"What the hell is going on, eh? Ordnance Inc. has lost a lot of people in the last twenty-four hours."

"The organization is having a bad streak of luck, but it won't affect us. Anyway, Healy wants me to meet him after we eliminate Tanner. I'm going to suggest they form more

Hammer Teams. If we had been down in Mexico that operation would have never fallen apart." Mitch checked his watch. "Steve, Kevin, wait fifteen minutes, then go outside and relieve Brian and Roberto. You'll have patrol until it's time to leave."

His men acknowledged his orders and Mitch went back to refining his attack plans. They were all unaware that they were being watched.

～

OUTSIDE, Tanner was lying on the ground and looking into the barn through a crack between two boards.

The interior was lit by battery-powered lanterns. The group's leader was seated at an improvised table made from sawhorses and a half sheet of plywood. The man was working on a computer tablet.

The waitress was seated across from her team leader and going through the contents of a backpack. She was locked in concentration as she rearranged items.

The remaining members of the team were four young men, one of whom was the waitress' pretend boyfriend.

One man had a weapon disassembled for cleaning, while the other three played cards. The card players sat on old metal buckets while using an empty wire reel for a table. Other than the man off to the side cleaning the weapon, they were all lined up in a narrow zone.

Tanner had taken the AR-15 from the sentry who'd been carving into the tree. The weapon had a fifty-round drum and had been modified with an attachment that would enable it to fire at full-auto.

Tanner twisted the knob on the stock to make the adjustment, stood, took three paces to the left, then dropped down to one knee.

All six targets were sitting, which placed their torsos approximately two to four feet from the ground. In his mind's eye, Tanner imagined his targets beyond the wooden wall.

~

INSIDE THE BARN, Scarlett turned her head to ask Mitch a question and watched as blood erupted from Mitch's chest. In the same instant, she became aware of the gunfire and the screams of her friends. She had only enough time to twitch before letting loose her own scream.

A round entered her right arm and exited out her biceps. That same arm was struck again, as a second bullet shattered her elbow. The pain was blinding, epic, and Scarlett felt herself passing out.

~

AFTER TANNER FINISHED EMPTYING the drum on the AR-15 he dived back to the spot where he had been looking through the crack.

The first thing he saw was the team leader. The man was on his back, his features twisted by extreme pain. Blood leaked from several wounds and the floor beneath him was turning crimson.

The waitress was just as bloody, and possibly dead, as it appeared she wasn't moving. Two of the three men who'd been playing cards were dead, their chests and necks had taken many rounds.

The third man lived, but not for long. He was on the floor, repeatedly grabbing fistfuls of hay, then releasing them.

He had taken a round to the forehead that miraculously

hadn't penetrated his skull, however, the ricocheting round had split his head open. His traumatized brain was swelling rapidly and seeping through the cracked skull.

Tanner had been most concerned about the man who'd been cleaning the weapon, but that worry proved to be unfounded. He had sent the last rounds from the AR-15 into the area were the man was seated. Those bullets had all struck him in the stomach. He must have frozen up when the firing began.

After using the night-vision monocular to check for more hostiles, Tanner entered the barn with a Glock leading the way.

He stood over the team leader and saw recognition light the man's watery eyes.

"How?" the man gasped.

Tanner didn't bother to respond. The answer was obvious. He was better than they were.

He stripped the dying man of his weapons and took his phone. As he did so, he watched the waitress, who had begun to stir back to consciousness.

Tanner went to her, evaluated her wounds, then lifted her up and laid her atop the table. Her wounds were not fatal. He took her weapon and moved on to the man with the head wound, who was still grabbing and releasing fistfuls of hay. Tanner slit his throat.

When he returned to the table, Scarlett was staring at him. The terror in her eyes was palpable, and she was crying.

"Oh shit, shit, shit."

"The waitress uniform with the diner name tag, was that real?"

"What?"

"You heard me."

"It's real. Mitch said it had to be real, because you can't fake that greasy spoon smell."

"And the waitress?"

Scarlett averted her eyes, and Tanner knew that they must have killed the real waitress.

"She's in the trunk of that car, isn't she?"

"Yeah, nah, but I didn't want to kill her. That was not my idea."

"Trevor Healy. Who is he?"

"If I tell you what you want to know will you let me live?"

Tanner tapped her wounded elbow with the butt of his gun. Scarlett cried out in agony.

"Trevor Healy," Tanner said.

"He's a coordinator. He runs the operations."

"How high up in the organization is he?"

"High. After the six coordinators, there's only the CEO."

"And who's the CEO?"

A look of displeasure flickered across Scarlett's face.

"He's an asshole named Grayson Talbot."

"You've met him?"

"Only once. I had to sleep with him if I wanted to be on a Hammer Team."

"I don't care about that. Tell me what he looks like."

"He's tall, about forty, with dark hair. He's nothing special to look at."

"What else can you tell me?"

Scarlett winced as she reached across her body with her good arm to grip Tanner's hand.

"I want to live, Tanner. Look at me. Do you like what you see? We can make a trade here, right?"

"Wrong."

Scarlett's tears increased, and she released Tanner's hand.

"I don't want to die."

"Neither did the waitress."

"Please, Tanner... I'm, I'm just a girl."

Those were to be Scarlett's last words.

178

24

TEDIOUS

ON HIS WAY BACK TO THE REYES RANCH, TANNER SPOTTED A police cruiser creeping along the road. The officer had likely heard the rounds fired from the AR-15 and was trying to figure out where the sound had originated. After making a second pass and checking things out with his searchlight, the officer drove on.

Ten minutes after Tanner had changed and showered, Thomas Lawson arrived with what he called a clean-up crew. They would dispose of the Hammer Team and their belongings. Lawson looked sickened by the news when Tanner told him about the waitress the team had killed.

"Ordnance Inc. was barely on my radar before yesterday, now they've made my top ten list."

"Because of what they did to Mr. White?"

"Yes, and you too, Tanner."

Tanner offered Lawson his hand.

"Call me when you want someone dead. I owe you more than one."

TANNER CALLED Sara's phone to leave her a message, but she picked up despite the early hour.

"Tanner?"

"It's me, and I'm in one piece."

Sara released a relieved sigh.

"No one knows better than I do how indestructible you are, but I still worry about you."

"I'm glad."

"Are you on your way here?"

"No, and it'll be a while yet. I've a breakfast meeting to attend."

~

6:58 A.M.

TREVOR HEALY STEPPED out of the rear of a Mercedes as his chauffeur held open the door for him. Standing beside the chauffeur was a bodyguard. Both men wore the Ordnance Inc. uniform of a black suit, red tie, beard, and mirrored sunglasses.

Healy's suit was a charcoal hue and his face was clean-shaven. He was above such things.

They were in the parking lot of a chain restaurant. The driver stayed with the car while the bodyguard accompanied Healy inside. As Healy took a seat at a corner booth, the bodyguard got two coffees to go.

With the coffee in hand, the bodyguard walked over to Healy's table.

"I'll bring Jack a coffee and be right back, sir."

Healy waved him off.

"Go sit with Jack, Gary. I need to talk with Mitch alone."

"Okay, just holler if you need me."

"Right," Healy said, as the waitress came over.

Healy ordered a cup of coffee and informed her that he was expecting someone. He had grabbed a newspaper on his way inside. After the waitress returned with the coffee, Trevor unfolded the newspaper and couldn't believe what he was seeing.

A photo of nine men and one woman showed them laid out on a tile floor. They were side by side with their arms crossed over their chests. The men were all bearded, wore mirrored sunglasses, and had black suits and red ties. Healy thought he recognized four of them.

The headline above the photo asked a question.

SUICIDE CULT IN DALLAS?

As he read the story, Healy learned that all ten had died from drinking poisoned beer laced with sedatives.

He was so engrossed in the story that he wasn't aware of Tanner until the assassin slid into the booth to settle across from him.

Healy looked up from the newspaper and his mouth fell open. As he struggled to compose himself, he gazed out into the parking lot. He had been hoping to see help on the way.

His car was still there, as were the bodyguard and chauffeur. Both men were slumped in their seats. They looked as still as stones. Healy knew that behind the men's mirrored sunglasses were eyes that would never see again.

Healy chuckled nervously.

"The Hammer Team, Mitch and his crew... all dead?"

Tanner answered with a nod.

Healy held up the newspaper and pointed at the picture.

"Was this you as well?"

Tanner stifled the urge to smile as he took in the photo. It looked as if Billy Price had kept their deal.

He ignored Healy's question and greeted the approaching waitress.

"I'll only be having coffee, but Healy here will have scrambled eggs and wheat toast."

The waitress thanked Tanner, poured coffee into a second cup, and went off to place the order.

Healy cleared his throat.

"You ordered me a meal. I hope that means you're going to let me live long enough to eat it?"

"It stops here, Healy."

"Yes, of course."

Tanner sighed. He should kill Healy, and kill Healy's boss, Grayson Talbot, while eradicating as many of Ordnance Inc.'s troops as he could. That would be the smart move.

There was just one problem. Tanner didn't want to do it.

He had nothing to prove. His reputation as a killing machine was well known. He didn't want to spend the next few days or weeks hunting down Ordnance Inc.'s red tie amateurs. He wanted to spend that time getting to know his brother.

Against his better judgment and experience, Tanner decided to issue a warning rather than make war. He hoped it never came back to bite him on the ass.

"Healy, in the past several years, I've taken down The Conglomerate, the Alvarado cartel, and The Brotherhood. I didn't give a damn about any of them at first, but they just kept coming at me. Believe me when I tell you I'm sick and tired of killing you people. It's getting tedious. I'm a paid assassin, Healy. It pisses me off when I have to work for free. That said, if I ever see a bearded clown in a black suit coming after me again I'll burn Ordnance Inc. to the ground."

Healy reached for his cup, then paused. His hand was shaking.

"Nothing we do is personal, Tanner. We're simply hired help."

"Moss Murphy hired you?"

"Yes."

"Where can I find him?"

"I don't know, I swear, but he should be calling any moment for news."

"If that happens, hand me the phone."

The food came. As the waitress was freshening their coffee cups, Healy's phone rang. He answered it as the waitress was walking away.

"Yes?"

"Is he dead?" asked an anxious Moss Murphy.

Healy handed the phone to Tanner.

"Murphy, this is Tanner."

There was silence. It was followed by a question that was asked in a whiny voice.

"Why are you so fucking hard to kill?"

"I'm coming, Murphy. Hide under any rock you choose and I'll find you."

The call ended.

Tanner tossed the phone at Healy and slid out of the booth.

"Remember what I said, Healy."

"I will, but you need to understand something, Tanner. It wasn't personal."

Tanner leaned over until his face was only inches from Healy's. Healy met his fierce gaze for an instant before breaking eye contact.

"Say that to me again and I'll kill you."

Healy was looking down at the table, where the trembling in his hands had increased.

"I'm sorry, Tanner. You'll never hear from us again."

There was no response. Healy looked up just in time to

see Tanner heading out the front doors of the restaurant. He pushed his plate away and walked toward the restroom on wobbly legs.

~

INSIDE THE DALLAS/FORT Worth International Airport, Finn Kelly found himself taking in a familiar face. He was not alone in observing the huge man, as his presence was a hard sight to ignore.

It was the Irish Hulk. He was sitting on a sofa meant to seat three comfortably, but was filling the couch quite nicely by himself. Although the Irish Hulk was seated, he still looked taller than most of the men walking past him.

Finn Kelly watched him for a while before approaching him. He had been hoping that Moss Murphy might be nearby, but no, the Irish Hulk seemed to be alone. He also looked dejected and was staring down at the floor.

"How are you, Banan?" Finn asked.

Banan O'Leary raised his massive head to look at Finn. His broad young face was lineless and devoid of guile. He smiled at Finn, but then looked worried.

"Moss said that you work for Joe Pullo now."

"That's true."

"Are you here to hurt me, Finn?"

Kelly smiled.

"Of course not, but what are you doing here, lad?"

"Moss left me here. He said he wasn't coming back."

"Did he return to Boston?"

"I don't think so, or he would have taken me with him. I think he's just gone somewhere to hide from that guy Tanner."

"Ah, and what about you? Are you going back to Boston?"

"I don't have a ticket or even any money. Moss always kept my money, you know, for safekeeping."

Kelly silently cursed Murphy for taking advantage of the simple kid. It was bad enough that Moss had always used the boy as a human shield to hide behind. He didn't need to cheat him as well.

"Follow me, lad. I'll get you a ticket that will take you back to Boston."

Banan lit up in a grin.

"Really? Thanks, Finn. I didn't know what I was going to do."

Kelly bought a ticket to Boston, actually two tickets, since Banan was too large for one seat. When he learned the man was hungry, it cost him another twenty dollars to feed him. On top of that he added cab fare for when Banan returned to Boston.

If Finn ever saw Moss Murphy again he planned to take the money out of his hide.

After Banan's flight left, Finn hung around the airport for another few hours. He had been hoping to come across Michael and Kate Barlow, but like Moss Murphy, the couple had gone into hiding.

He took out his phone and called Joe Pullo. After filling Pullo in on the news about Moss Murphy, Finn asked Joe if he still wanted him to pursue the couple that robbed him.

"Do you think you could track them down?"

"Possibly, but it won't be easy and it'll take some time."

There was a pause in the conversation as Pullo considered things. When he spoke again, Finn heard the resolve in his tone.

"Yeah, Finn. Stay on them. Those two need to learn a lesson about messing with the wrong people."

"I'll call Bosco with an update every day."

"Do that, and stay safe."

When the call ended, Finn went to a bar inside the terminal. He had a drink as he thought over everything he'd learned about Michael and Kate Barlow. He knew damn little, but a smile crept across his face when he realized he might know enough about them after all.

Kelly finished his drink. Two hours later, he was in the air and headed south.

25

FAMILY

S TARK EXTENDED HIS TRIP TO T EXAS SO THAT HE AND T ANNER could get to know each other better. The two brothers spent some of that time together tending to the graves of their family.

Although Stark hadn't grown up on the ranch as Tanner had, he had been raised on a farm after his mother's death. Neither man was a stranger to hard physical labor.

They dug the holes, mixed the cement, and erected a wrought iron fence around the headstones. There was also a gate that locked. More cameras were added to join the ones Thomas Lawson had installed, and the Parker family cemetery was under video surveillance 24/7.

When the work was completed, Tanner handed Stark a cold beer he'd taken from a cooler, then opened one for himself. The two brothers sat beside each other on the open tailgate of a pickup truck and stared through the bars at the graves.

"Cody?"

"Yeah."

"I want to thank you for understanding about our Mom."

"You're welcome, but I agree. It wouldn't be right to move her."

Marian Gant Parker had been laid to rest on the farm belonging to Caleb Parker's adoptive father. She had passed away in her sleep. Her last words to Caleb were a wish that he be a good man.

A second grave for Marian Parker was inside the Parker cemetery. There was no longer a body in it, and what unfortunate soul had once filled it was a mystery. It was thought that Billy Gant, Tanner and Stark's deceased uncle, had likely murdered a prostitute to substitute for his sister.

Stark lifted his head up as a thought occurred to him.

"The owner of the ranch, this Mrs. Reyes, you got her permission to do all this, right?"

"Maria and I had a long talk a few days ago. I helped her once with a problem she had and she trusts me. I decided to trust her and tell her who I really am. Not the assassin part, but she now knows that I'm Cody Parker."

"How did she take that?"

"She said she felt horrible about everything that happened to me on the night of the... when Alvarado was here. I also told her about you, and that I had a brother."

Stark smiled.

"I'm still getting used to having a brother, but I like it."

Tanner smiled back at him, and they tapped their beer bottles together. Then, Tanner had a question.

"Did you take your adoptive father's surname of Knox because it would be safer for you? If so, it was a good idea. As insane as Alvarado was, if he'd learned of your existence he might have wanted you dead."

Stark finished his beer, then he began peeling back the label on the bottle by using his thumbnail. Tanner recalled that their father used to do the same thing to his beer bottles.

"As far as I knew, Cody, I was the last of my kind. I was

just a kid, but I wanted to hold onto my name. I didn't though, because it might have placed my adopted family at risk."

"You can always change it back if you want. I would take mine back as well, but that would lead to too many damn questions."

"I took Stark as an alias to honor the town our family helped to build. When Mom and I were riding the bus out of here years ago, that old water tower with the word STARK in big letters was the last sight of the town I saw. But I never forgot where I came from, even though I thought I could never come back here."

Tanner grunted.

"In a way, Moss Murphy did me a favor. If not for him, we may have never known we were brothers."

They drank another beer before cleaning up after themselves and loading their tools into the rear of the pickup.

"I told Doc I'd fix a leaning fence post for him," Tanner said.

"I do that on the farm in California. We don't raise horses, but we have a few."

"Have you seen the whole ranch, Caleb?"

"No."

"It's small by Texas standards, but every acre has been in our family for generations… and it's going to stay there."

"What's that mean?"

"I'm buying the ranch from Maria Reyes. I want to put the property in your name."

"My name?"

"You're a Parker."

Tanner spotted the loose fence post Doc had mentioned. They still had some cement left, so he decided to mix up a little in the wheelbarrow and use it to fortify the post. Stark steadied the post as Tanner used a trowel to spread the mixture.

"Cody, I don't mean to sound ungrateful, but I don't want to live here. Don't get me wrong. I would love to keep this land in the family, but I have responsibilities in California."

"I get that, kid. Don't panic. I'm not trying to rearrange your life. You'll own the ranch, but nothing will change. Doc will stay on as caretaker and Maria has a year to vacate. Part of this was Maria's idea. She said she'd feel guilty keeping the land now that she knows Frank Parker had heirs."

"Yeah?"

"Yes."

"Oh, and you really have enough money to buy the ranch?"

"Maria is giving us a great deal. Even so, I'll be just about tapped out."

"I have some money and I can always get more."

"By robbing crooks?"

"It pays well."

"It's dangerous."

"Look who's talking. Even your girlfriend has tried to kill you."

Tanner had been smoothing out the cement. He looked up and smiled.

"I see you and Sara have been talking."

"She's awesome. If you don't marry her, I will."

"She's taken," Tanner said. He stood and told Stark to let go of the post. It seemed firm, but Tanner cut a length of rope to wrap around it. The ends were each attached to a neighboring fencepost so that the post wouldn't lean while the cement set.

Tanner walked to the truck and climbed in, then saw that Stark was still standing outside the passenger door and looking around.

"What's wrong?"

"I'm really going to own this ranch?"

Tanner went to his brother. Stark's resemblance to their late father had registered with Tanner when he'd first met the man. At the time, Stark had been wearing a three-piece suit. In a pair of well-worn jeans and a cowboy hat, Tanner felt the resemblance remarkable.

Tanner leaned his back against the truck, and Stark settled beside him.

"Maria is returning here for Thanksgiving. If you come back here sometime during that week, you and she can start the process. Within a short time, the ranch will belong to the Parker family again. I suspect you'll be considered a big deal in Stark if you ever let on who you are. Our ancestors help found this community."

"Cody?"

"Yeah?"

"Tell me about our family. What was our father like? And our sisters, what was it like to have sisters?"

Tanner swallowed once, twice, then answered in a voice thick with emotion.

"I loved them all, Caleb… and I let them down when they needed me the most."

"You're talking about the massacre? Cody, you were just a teenager and they were an army."

Tanner broke eye contact.

"I let you down too."

"I don't understand."

"Moss Murphy wanted to torture me. He gave me a choice, knowing that no matter what I did, I would lose. It turned out to be a trap, but I didn't know that. I had only enough time to save one of you and… Caleb… I chose Sara."

"I don't blame you for that. You're in love with Sara. Besides, I can take care of myself, big brother."

"Yes, I've noticed that."

They climbed back in the truck and moved along the fence line. An old memory of their mother came to Tanner, prompting him to ask his brother a question.

"Do you like asparagus?"

"I think it's nasty."

"So did our mother and father, but I love the taste. Our mother used to grow asparagus in her greenhouse, even though I was the only one that ate it."

"Mom always had a garden, and she always grew asparagus in it. Now I know why."

"I miss her, Caleb."

"So do I, Cody, so do I."

∼

THAT NIGHT, Tanner was standing on the front porch of the ranch house and staring out at the moonlit landscape. As he stood there, he recalled many nights spent on a similar porch with his family. The home was different, but the land was the same. And soon, it would be Parker land once more.

Sara came out onto the porch with a sweater on. She was walking stiffly, having overindulged in horseback riding.

She had loved it as a girl, but hadn't done it for years, being at the ranch she took up the habit again.

Sara greeted Tanner with a kiss, then leaned into him as he placed an arm around her.

"It's so beautiful and peaceful here," Sara said.

"When I was a kid I couldn't wait to go off and see the world, but I always planned to come back here to live. I've seen the world, but until now I never thought I'd ever live here again."

"You want to live here?"

"Maybe someday."

"It must have been a great place for a boy to grow up."

Tanner nodded.

"It was."

"I love New York, but I could see myself living here. I'd forgotten how much I loved the outdoors."

They grew silent, but then Sara had a question as she gazed up at him.

"What are you thinking about? For a moment, your face had such a blissful expression."

Tanner pulled Sara into an embrace.

"I'm happy, as happy as I've been in a very long time."

"Because of your brother?"

"Yes, but it's more than having discovered Caleb, there's being with you, and this land, Sara. I hadn't realized how much owning this land would mean to me. It will be in Caleb's name only, but this will once more be the Parker Ranch. That means a hell of a lot to me."

Sara grinned.

"Welcome home, Cody Parker."

Tanner looked out at the land and sighed.

"It's damn good to be back."

EPILOGUE

TREVOR HEALY STEPPED OFF A PRIVATE ELEVATOR INSIDE AN office building in Chicago. He wondered if he would be alive for very long.

It was night, and he was meeting with Ordnance Inc.'s CEO, Grayson Talbot. Talbot had been far from pleased by the disasters that had occurred under Healy's area of responsibility.

Between the operations that had taken place in Texas and Mexico, Ordnance Inc. had lost dozens of men, thousands in equipment, and two Hammer Teams. Remarkably, the predominant damage came as a result of crossing just two men, Tanner and Mr. White.

In the Mexican debacle, where Mr. White was involved, Healy had suffered a personal loss as well. His girlfriend, a woman named Caitlin Wards, had been killed. Healy hadn't been in love with Caitlin, but he had liked her. It grated on him that the person who killed her would never be punished for it.

He exhaled loudly. What did it matter? He would likely

soon be dead as well. He had failed miserably. Grayson Talbot was not a man who forgave failure.

Why the hell am I here? Healy asked himself. *I should have packed a bag and run.*

That option dissolved as Grayson Talbot opened an office door that was flanked by two armed bodyguards. After staring at Healy, Talbot motioned for Healy to enter.

As Scarlett had told Tanner, Grayson Talbot was tall, about forty, with dark hair. Talbot never wore suits. He wore black slacks with long-sleeved turtleneck shirts. When needed due to the weather, a black leather coat went over the ensemble. It was like a uniform. Healy had never seen the man wear anything else.

They had spoken once on the phone since Healy's return to Chicago, and Healy had sent over a full report of what had occurred. That detailed statement was atop Talbot's desk in the form of an encrypted flash drive. Healy took a seat across from his boss and waited to learn his fate.

Talbot pushed back the sleeves of his shirt, then poked a stiff finger at the flash drive.

"We need to make changes in the organization."

Healy said nothing, which prompted Talbot to cock an eyebrow.

"You disagree?"

"Um, no sir. There are changes that might be made. I was just wondering if my dismissal was one of them."

"Dismissal? Trevor, if I was going to dismiss you I wouldn't hold a meeting about it. You'd already be dead."

Healy released a long breath.

"Thank you, sir. I'd like a chance to redeem myself."

"You'll have it, because I can see what happened wasn't your fault. The problem is that we're not set up to handle men like this Tanner and Mr. White. Our focus was on customer service, but we need to place more emphasis on self-preservation."

"You have some ideas?"

"It's simple; we need to get bigger and badder. If Tanner had faced the equivalent of ten Hammer Teams even he wouldn't have survived."

"Are you talking about building an army?"

"I am, and I'll be placing you in charge of recruitment. To fund the operation, I'll concentrate on bringing in more business."

"What happens once we have everything in place? I think we'll be in a position then to offer our services to the world market."

"Exactly, but before that happens, there will be a first order of business—revenge."

"Against Tanner?"

Talbot smiled. Healy thought it was like watching a shark grin.

"That bastard did us a lot of damage and made a direct threat to eliminate us. We'll bide our time, Trevor. We'll get stronger, then we'll hit that son of a bitch with everything we've got."

Healy was pleased with the plan. Tanner had instilled fear in him, had made him feel like less than a man during their confrontation. It would be a pleasure to see the assassin dead.

"When the time comes, I'll personally bring you Tanner's head, sir. It will be my pleasure."

～

RIO DE JANEIRO, BRAZIL

THE COUPLE who had once been known as Michael and Kate Barlow were in the city for a day of shopping. They had changed identities three times in the last several weeks. The final time, they both had facelifts, dyed their hair blond, and began wearing clothes that someone of a younger age might wear.

The result made them look more youthful than they previously appeared. They were confident that they had eluded anyone who might have been on their trail.

Michael, who was going by the name Christopher, opened the trunk of their pre-owned BMW and loaded their packages. Kate, who was using the name Brittany, drove. During the trip, they listened to a language tape. They were planning on staying in Brazil for a while and wanted to learn to speak Portuguese.

Their rented home was secluded and had its own beachfront. It was quite a drive from the city, but it mattered little. They would only venture into Rio on rare occasions. As they were approaching their new home, the man who had been known as Michael Barlow used his phone to check the security cameras. The home was small, so it only took six interior cameras and three exterior cameras to cover everything.

Confident that no one was lurking about ready to pounce on them, they continued toward the house.

~

THE COUPLE AWOKE with a start nine hours later. It was well after midnight and they had been sleeping in the nude after having made love. Someone was shining a powerful flashlight at them.

They groped for the weapons they kept on their

nightstands, then moaned in unison as a voice told them not to bother. Their guns were no longer there.

The voice had a distinctive Irish lilt. It was the voice of Finn Kelly.

Kelly wore a headlamp which left his hands free. Those hands were holding a Mossberg pump-action shotgun.

The woman, who Finn knew as Kate Barlow, began crying.

"How did you find us? There's no way Joe Pullo could have tracked us down," Kate said.

"I found your picture weeks ago on a security camera at a travel agency. You were looking in their window right before you robbed Pullo. You had been staring at travel ads extoling the beauty of Brazil. I've been in Rio for weeks trying to locate you. By the way, Kate, you looked better as a brunette."

Michael Barlow swung his feet to the floor.

Finn said, "Ah-ah," and Michael placed his hands in the air.

"Please, let me talk to Joe Pullo," Michael said. "We have skills that a man like Pullo could use. If you kill us, all he gets is revenge."

"There's nothing wrong with revenge," Finn said. "And yet, Mr. Pullo was of the same mind. He has a task for you. If you can complete it in a short time he'll let you live."

Kate had the covers pulled up to her neck. Finn knew there were no weapons hidden under there. He had peeked beneath the covers before waking the couple.

"What does Pullo want us to do?"

Finn smiled at her.

"You'll do what you do best. You'll find someone who doesn't want to be found."

"Who?"

"Your former employer, a man named Moss Murphy."

"If we find Murphy, Joe Pullo will let us live?"

"He will."

"Tanner," Michael said. "What about Tanner?"

Finn gave a little shrug.

"That's a kettle of fish from a different pond. However, if you were to become valued associates of Tanner's good friend Mr. Pullo, Tanner might be more inclined to let you two keep breathing."

Michael hung his head.

"We go to work for Joe Pullo or we die."

Finn smiled.

"Now you got it, boy-o."

~

CALGARY, ALBERTA, EIGHT DAYS LATER

Moss Murphy returned to the small home he was renting and headed to the kitchen to make himself a drink.

Bodyguards, chauffeurs, and maids were a thing of the past. Murphy figured if he laid low and stayed out of trouble he wouldn't show up on anyone's radar.

Calgary was a city of over a million people with a population that was fifteen percent Irish. He was more than two thousand miles from New York City and had cut all ties with Boston. If was tough to walk away from everyone and everything you knew, but it was better than dying.

Murphy became lost in thought as he sipped his drink, while leaning back against the refrigerator. Going after Tanner had been a gamble, which he had lost badly.

In his absence from Boston, one of his men had taken over. Murphy didn't dare attempt to take his position back. If he did so, Tanner would be in Boston to greet him.

Murphy wore a lopsided smile. Things weren't so bad.

His son Liam was safe, he was safe, and he had more than enough money to live a good life in Calgary.

Many men like himself had ended far worse. A lot of them had died young or were wasting away in prison. He even had a date coming up with a woman he'd met at the park. Murphy looked up at the clock above the stove and finished his drink.

He was supposed to pick up his date soon, but he still needed to shave, shower, and change clothes. He left the kitchen, walked through the living room, and entered the bedroom.

When he saw Tanner sitting by the window, his shoulders slumped as a moan escaped his lips. He would never have that date.

"How the hell did you find me?"

Tanner was holding a gun. Attached to the weapon was one of the silencers created by the man Duke said was a former CIA toymaker. Tanner fired and hit Murphy in the right knee. The gun made little noise. The suppressors were single use, so as Murphy collapsed to the floor, Tanner used his gloved hands to exchange the spent one for a new one.

He walked over and stared down at Murphy.

"Liam's next."

Murphy gazed up at him with pleading eyes.

"Don't kill me! Please don't fucking kill me."

"You can't be serious."

"No, no, listen, Tanner. I can make you richer than you've ever dreamed. Come back to Boston with me and I'll cut you in on all the profits." Murphy stopped talking and groaned from the pain of his wound. When he spoke again, his words came faster and reeked of desperation. "We can make a deal, right? I'm serious here. I can make you rich."

"I don't want your money. I want you dead."

Tanner aimed his weapon at Murphy and watched the

man raise his hands in front of his face, as if he could ward off a bullet.

"No! No, wait. I can find Liam for you. I swear I'll find out where he is, but I have to be alive to do it."

"What are you telling me, that you'll give up your own son if I let you live?"

Self-loathing welled-up in Murphy. It was shoved aside by anger and the will to live.

"Yes, damn it! This whole thing started with Liam. He never should have tried to kill you and Pullo."

"But he did, and you backed his play. Now it's time to face the consequences."

Murphy's face scrunched up. Tears of self-pity flowed from eyes already wet with pain.

"I shouldn't have to die, Tanner. None of this was my fault. Can't you see that? Every bit of this was caused by Liam."

Tanner was done talking. He shot Moss Murphy in the chest and watched him die.

~

HOURS LATER, Sara smiled as Tanner joined her on the shore of Lake Minnewanka. Beyond the lake and above the Cascade Mountain, the aurora borealis was putting on quite a display.

Before joining her, Tanner had stood behind a crowd of sky gazers and watched Sara. He had been willing to sacrifice a brother for her. That he loved her hadn't been in doubt, but the depth of his love had surprised him.

Sara had dropped everything and run off to Texas when he needed her. She had been threatened with death because she was with him.

She hadn't complained, or been disheartened, or

questioned the wisdom of staying with him. She had been the same tough, resilient woman who had once bested him. Tanner didn't doubt that she would stand by him no matter what.

He saw delight in Sara's eyes as he took her in his arms, then felt joy and peace fill his own heart. It had nothing to do with the majesty of the mountain or the wonder of the northern lights. It was the fact that he was there with Sara Blake.

Sara glanced skyward to view the heavenly display of lights.

"It's so beautiful."

"So are you," Tanner said, and kissed her.

It was at that moment that he knew he would marry her.

JOIN MY INNER CIRCLE

You'll receive FREE books, such as,

SLAY BELLS – A TANNER NOVEL – BOOK 0
    TAKEN! ALPHABET SERIES – 26 ORIGINAL TAKEN!
TALES
    BLUE STEELE – FIRST CAPTURE
    CALIBER DETECTIVE AGENCY – EARLY DAYS

Also – Exclusive short stories featuring TANNER, along with many other books.

TO BECOME AN INNER CIRCLE MEMBER, GO TO:
    http://remingtonkane.com/mailing-list/

The TAKEN! Series in order

TAKEN! - LOVE CONQUERS ALL - Book 1
TAKEN! - SECRETS & LIES - Book 2
TAKEN! - STALKER - Book 3
TAKEN! - BREAKOUT! - Book 4
TAKEN! - THE THIRTY-NINE - Book 5
TAKEN! - KIDNAPPING THE DEVIL - Book 6
TAKEN! - HIT SQUAD - Book 7
TAKEN! - MASQUERADE - Book 8
TAKEN! - SERIOUS BUSINESS - Book 9
TAKEN! - THE COUPLE THAT SLAYS TOGETHER - Book 10
TAKEN! - PUT ASUNDER - Book 11
TAKEN! - LIKE BOND, ONLY BETTER - Book 12
TAKEN! - MEDIEVAL - Book 13
TAKEN! - RISEN! - Book 14
TAKEN! - VACATION - Book 15
TAKEN! - MICHAEL - Book 16
TAKEN! - BEDEVILED - Book 17
TAKEN! - INTENTIONAL ACTS OF VIOLENCE - Book 18
TAKEN! - THE KING OF KILLERS – Book 19
TAKEN! - NO MORE MR. NICE GUY

The BLUE STEELE Series in order

BLUE STEELE - BOUNTY HUNTER- Book 1

BLUE STEELE - BROKEN- Book 2

BLUE STEELE - VENGEANCE- Book 3

BLUE STEELE - THAT WHICH DOESN'T KILL ME- Book 4

BLUE STEELE - ON THE HUNT- Book 5

BLUE STEELE - PAST SINS - Book 6

The CALIBER DETECTIVE AGENCY Series in order

CALIBER DETECTIVE AGENCY - GENERATIONS- Book 1

CALIBER DETECTIVE AGENCY - TEMPTATION- Book 2

CALIBER DETECTIVE AGENCY - A RANSOM PAID IN BLOOD- Book 3

CALIBER DETECTIVE AGENCY - MISSING- Book 4

CALIBER DETECTIVE AGENCY - DECEPTION- Book 5

CALIBER DETECTIVE AGENCY - CRUCIBLE- Book 6

CALIBER DETECTIVE AGENCY – LEGENDARY – Book 7

CALIBER DETECTIVE AGENCY – WE ARE GATHERED HERE TODAY - Book 8

ALSO

THE EFFECT: Reality is changing!

THE CONTRACT: KILL JESSICA WHITE - Taken!/Tanner - Book 1

UNFINISHED BUSINESS – Taken!/Tanner – Book 2

Made in the USA
Middletown, DE
23 November 2017